SHORT STORIES

Illustrated by
Tapas Guha

Children's Book Trust, New Delhi

These stories are a collection made from entries in the Competition for Writers of Children's Books organized by Children's Book Trust.

EDITED BY BHAVANA NAIR

Text typeset in 12/16 pt. Bookman Old Style

© by CBT 1999
Reprinted 2000

ISBN 81-7011-843-3

Published by Children's Book Trust and printed at its Indraprastha Press, Nehru House, 4 Bahadur Shah Zafar Marg, New Delhi.

CONTENTS

Our Next-Door Neighbour   5
Devika Rangachari

The Magic Carpet   12
Tithi Tavora

A Game Of Tennis   19
Dipavali Debroy

His Highness   26
Homagni Chaudhuri

Twin Trouble   32
Agila Girirajkumar

Grandad's Happy Hour   39
Neela Subramaniam

The House That Walked   45
Sarojine Chopra

Odd One In   52
Tithi Tavora

Nani's Football Match   58
Sudarshan Kumar Bhatia

The Land Of The Lost   64
Arati Luthra Pinto

One Step At A Time   69
Cheryl Rao

The Runaway Engine   76
Girija Rani Asthana

Roli And The Coin   82
Aradhna Jha

Ajji's Temporary Amnesia   88
Madhavi Mahadevan

My Father's Wife   95
Deepa Agarwal

Battle Of The Brains   102
Vandana Kumari Jena

The Shawl   108
Lata Kaku

Bholu   115
Vaneeta Vaid

A Soldier's Son   124
Shobha Ghose

A Different Diwali   130
Tithi Tavora

Upside Down Magic   136
Sonali Bhatia

Of Flowers And Flying   143
Through The Year
Brinda Gill

Our Next-Door Neighbour
Devika Rangachari

Ravi and I were looking idly out of our window when a truck drew up before the house next door.

"Someone is moving in!" I gasped. "What do we do?"

We stared at each other. The garden of that house had been our playground for the past month. We had spent many a happy hour hunting for 'treasures' in the tangled grass and playing hide-and-seek when we felt like it. We would often peer in through the smudged glass windows and wonder what the house was like inside.

"There is a ghost there," Ravi would say. "I can hear it!"

I would shudder and cross my fingers and utter a prayer to keep us safe. And now we would never be able to play there again. We would have to be content with our concrete driveway which fell to the lot of all corner houses in the neighbourhood.

It had been raining since morning and we were confined to the house.

"Watch them slip and slide all over the place," Ravi smirked. "There is wet mud there and their boxes will be a mess!"

I nodded with a certain grim satisfaction and peered at the

figures alighting from the truck. Then I stiffened and clutched Ravi's shoulder.

"That is Mr. Shankar!" I cried. "He is moving in next door! Oh, Ravi!"

My twin stared unbelieving at the tall, thin, bespectacled person who was ordering the packers around.

"Yes, it is," he said slowly. "My God!"

We stared, stupefied, at our mathematics teacher, the terror of our school, whose single word or glance was enough to send us scurrying for cover.

"He is right next door," I repeated. "Help! What do we do?"

We appealed to our parents. They were most unsympathetic.

"What is the problem?" grumbled our father. "You can't choose your neighbours in any case."

"You can ask him for help whenever you want," said our mother brightly. "You are always struggling with your maths. Now your problem is solved."

Ravi and I looked at each other and sighed. There was no use trying to explain the enormity of the situation to them. We found a more receptive audience in our friends.

"What a disaster!" cried Madhuri. "You poor things!"

"You will be at the same bus-stop," added Pradip with gloomy relish. "He will complain to your parents when you do badly..."

This aspect of the situation had not struck us earlier. We were in the doldrums for most of the day. We tried hard to concentrate in the mathematics class but the sight of Mr. Shankar's looming figure drove all thoughts of algebra out of our heads. It was when we alighted from the bus together that he looked mildly surprised.

"Do you live here?" he barked.

"Yes, Sir."

"We are your next-door neighbours, Sir," I ventured, quaking as I always did when he looked at me.

"I see," he said and strode rapidly away.

The following morning, we delayed going to the bus-stop. Ravi kept watch and finally announced, "There, he is leaving."

We lingered about, talking and taking our time until our mother got worried.

"You better go now," she said firmly. "You will miss the bus at this rate."

Just then Ravi saw the bus turning the corner; he and I sprinted to the bus-stop in record time. We did this five days in a row. Mr. Shankar cast us a disapproving look each time. When we dashed up, breathless and panting, on the sixth day, he frowned.

"Why can't you get to the bus-stop well in time?" he demanded sternly. "This is not the right thing to do."

We hung our heads meekly but knew we had to acknowledge defeat. After that we reported to the stop in time and had to spend agonizing moments alone with Mr. Shankar before we were released by the bus. He would ask us questions about our grades and clear his throat in a nasty manner every time we had low marks to report.

"You children don't study these days," he declared disgustedly one day. "You either want to watch TV or waste your time. Something should be done about this."

That decided me. "I am not coming out today," I told Ravi that evening.

"Why? We have done our homework."

"No! If you-know-who is on the prowl, I don't want to be caught wasting my time. What if he complains to someone?"

"But playing is good for health," argued Ravi. "Mr. Roy says so, you know that!" The last named was our PT teacher and Ravi's idol.

"No way," I said. "I am going to sit on the front steps and read so that he is impressed. You can do what you want."

A disgruntled Ravi walked out while I selected a thick textbook and sat studiously on the front steps. Fifteen minutes later,

7

when I was beginning to feel regretful of my stance, Ravi came along with a dog at his heels. We had seen this friendly, black creature wandering about the lanes and boldly exploring everyone's gardens. We had even seen him go next door and had prayed for his safety. I jumped down and patted him.

"You are a darling," I said. "Who do you belong to? Your collar isn't marked."

The dog wagged his tail frantically.

"He followed me," said Ravi proudly. "I think he likes me."

Then the gate clicked open and Mr. Shankar strode across the path towards us.

"God help us," muttered Ravi and I glanced guiltily at my textbook lying discarded on the top step.

"What are you doing..." he began.

Ravi nervously interrupted him. "Nothing, Sir. We were just going in to study, Sir. We..."

"Stop talking, boy, and listen to me," snapped Mr. Shankar. "That is my dog. I was wondering where he had got to."

We stared in amazement as the dog frolicked happily by his master's side and disappeared inside the house.

"Well!" said Ravi, the word dark with unspoken meaning.

I nodded.

"I bet he tortures the dog in there," I said. "There is no one to watch him or report him. No wonder the dog has sad eyes."

"Does he?" asked Ravi, interested. "How do you make that out? Are they like cows' eyes?" Ravi had been an animal lover ever since he learnt to distinguish cats from dogs.

"Children, what are you doing?" Our mother joined us outside. "I thought you said you had a test tomorrow. Maths, isn't it?"

"Yes," replied Ravi gloomily. "We have prepared for it. It is just silly old equations."

'The silly old equations' proved to be a real disaster for us the following day. Mr. Shankar seemed to have invented the toughest problems. Though we scratched our heads and sucked

8

our pens and balanced and simplified and teased the numbers about, the solution to them eluded us.

"Whew!" Madhuri rubbed her eyes after the class. "What a horrible, perverse test! You two must have annoyed him yesterday; he is taking revenge."

We were in for an ordeal when our papers were returned. All of us had failed and we quailed at the sight of Mr. Shankar's stormy expression, glinting eyes and angry tone.

"Useless, the lot of you!" he thundered. "I give you a simple test and you can't get one thing right!"

Ravi brooded about his marks all day. He fancied himself an amateur mathematics expert and it worried him to face failure of this sort. I decided to cheer him up.

"Come on, Ravi," I dragged him out in the evening. "It is ages since we played hide-and-seek."

"No," he said, "I..." He stopped short as sounds of screaming laughter assailed our ears. It was coming from the next door garden! Emboldened by curiosity, we rushed across to the fence and peered at what had been our private hunting-ground.

Mr. Shankar was rolling on the grass with a frisbee in his hands while his dog pranced around, trying to snatch it.

"He is laughing!" gasped Ravi.

I wondered if I was dreaming.

Mr. Shankar looked up just then and sprang to his feet. The sight of two interested observers must have disconcerted him. He fingered the frisbee in an embarrassed fashion and seemed to make up his mind.

"Want to join us?" he called.

Ravi recovered faster than I did.

"Yes, Sir," he answered and dragged me after him.

The dog ran up to us and licked our hands.

"Trigo likes you," Mr. Shankar remarked.

"Trigo?" I ventured.

"After trigonometry," he explained briefly. "Come on. You

10

stand there and I shall throw the frisbee to you."

An hour later we rushed home to collect our books.

"Where are you going?" asked our mother.

"Next door. Mr. Shankar is going to help us solve equations."

The Magic Carpet
Tithi Tavora

"Vicky! look at what you have done now!" yelled Divya. "Wait till Mummy sees it!"

Vicky looked guiltily at the big, red blob of paint he had spilt on their new carpet.

"Let us clean it before Mummy returns," he said.

"I shall do that for you!" said a voice.

Both children stopped in amazement. They stared at the carpet. The voice seemed to have come from there. Then, before their very eyes, the blob of paint was gone. Vanished! Just like that. Without either of them having done anything!

They were still staring when their mother walked in. "What are the two of you looking at?" she asked.

"Mummy, the carpet, it talks..." babbled Divya.

"It is a magic carpet," squealed Vicky.

"Divya, haven't I told you not to fill Vicky's head with your fanciful nonsense? Carpets that talk, what next!" exclaimed Mrs. Mehra, exasperated.

That evening the carpet spoke again.

They were watching a cricket match on television. Vicky's

12

eyes were glued to the TV as he dug into a bowl of chips.

"O-O-U-T!" he yelled, jumping up and down and dropping the chips in his excitement. Before he could pick them up, they were gone!

"M-m-m! Those were tasty!" said an appreciative voice.

"*Didi* (elder sister), the carpet, it is talking again," whispered Vicky, his voice trembling a bit.

Divya nodded. She had heard it too.

"Listen," she said, addressing the carpet, "who are you?"

"I am Aziz, one of the boys who made this carpet," came the clear reply.

"You sound like a small boy. How could you have made this carpet?" enquired Divya disbelievingly.

"There are children younger than me who do this work," replied Aziz sadly.

"Where?" asked Vicky.

"At the carpet factory, where I live," said Aziz.

"If you live there, how can your voice be here?" asked Divya.

"Well, you see, one day, when I was weaving this carpet, I began day-dreaming. I imagined that the people who bought this carpet would take me home, too. When your mother bought the carpet, my dream came along."

"Where are *you*? The *real* you?" persisted Vicky.

"Back at the factory."

"Aren't you happy there?" asked Vicky.

"Happy? We have to work from five in the morning till eight in the night, with only an hour's break for lunch. By the time we finish, we are too tired to play. We just drop off to sleep."

"You mean you don't go to school?" asked Vicky enviously.

"We would love to. But our parents are poor. They can't afford to feed us, leave alone send us to school. They sent us to work thinking we would be better off here. They don't know how badly we are treated. I wish I could go home!" sobbed the voice.

"*Didi*, Aziz is crying," said Vicky, close to tears himself.

"Don't cry, Aziz, we will help you. How can we meet you, the real you?" asked Divya.

"Well," replied Aziz uncertainly, "if you come to the factory you probably..." He fell silent. Mr. Mehra had entered the room.

Divya ran up to him. "We want to go to the carpet factory!"

"To meet Aziz!" interjected Vicky.

"The *real* Aziz!" emphasized Divya.

"Hey! What is all this? Who is Aziz?" asked their father, amused and puzzled.

"Aziz is the boy who made this carpet, Papa. This is a dream carpet, it talks to us..." Divya explained.

"Divya, I told you not to let your imagination run wild. This is going too far now!" scolded Mrs. Mehra.

"It is not my imagination," protested Divya. "Please Papa," she pleaded and proceeded to tell him Aziz's story.

He listened patiently. "Very well, we will go to meet your Aziz on Sunday," he agreed.

"You can't be serious about taking them to the carpet factory," said Mrs. Mehra incredulously. "This is one of Divya's fairy tales and she has convinced Vicky to believe it too."

"Even if it is, the visit won't harm them," argued Mr. Mehra.

The children could hardly wait till Sunday.

Aziz was excited too. "You will find me at the loom," he said. "Malik sahab does not allow anyone to see the looms because he doesn't want people to know that he employs children. However, if he thinks you will buy a carpet, he might agree."

The children told their father all this on the way to the factory.

Upon arrival, they were greeted by a fat, middle-aged man.

"He must be Malik," whispered Divya to Vicky.

"Welcome! Welcome! You would like to buy a carpet?" he gushed, leading them into a room where carpets of all sizes and colours were displayed.

After inspecting a few, Mrs. Mehra said, "My children would like to see how these carpets are made. Can you show us?"

A guarded look came over the man's face.

Mrs. Mehra cleverly stroked a red carpet. "This one is nice," she said, smiling at Mr. Mehra.

The owner's face lit up. "Yes, yes, madam, you have a good choice!" He began unrolling it.

"We will decide on it later," said Mrs. Mehra, "after we see the loom."

The man hesitated. He seemed reluctant, yet, if it meant clinching a sale...

"Of course! My pleasure! Come this way!" he exclaimed finally.

He led them across the courtyard through a narrow door into a dimly-lit room. After the bright sunlight outside, they could hardly see anything inside. Gradually, they made out the shapes of enormous looms. Sitting and working in front of them were at least twenty children. There was wool fluff everywhere. Vicky started coughing.

"This is our factory," said the owner proudly.

"These children? Isn't it against the law to employ them?" asked Mr. Mehra grimly.

"Law, sahab? Will the law feed them? I am looking after them. At home they would go hungry!" replied the man pompously.

Meanwhile, Vicky and Divya searched the faces of the children. Most of them were eight to twelve years old. They seemed afraid, though some smiled shyly at them.

Seeing that they had stopped work, Malik shouted at them, "Carry on with your work! Don't waste time!"

The children resumed knotting and cutting wool. All except one thin, dark, boy of about ten who kept staring at them.

Divya went up to him. "Aziz?" she asked hopefully.

The boy nodded, looking startled.

"Don't you know us? Your dream has brought us to you."

A slow smile spread across the boy's face. "You came, you actually came!" He could not seem to believe his eyes.

Seeing them talking to the boy, Mrs. Mehra came up to them.

15

"Who is this, Divya?" she asked curiously.

"Mummy, this is Aziz who spoke to us through the carpet."

Mrs. Mehra looked at Aziz in amazement. "Did you really speak to them?"

Aziz looked down. "I just spoke to myself. I often do that at work, especially when I think of home."

Mrs. Mehra gently took Aziz's hands in hers, gasping at the deep cuts on them.

"We get those from cutting the wool," he explained, wincing.

"Where is your home?" enquired Mrs. Mehra.

"In Bihar. Malik brought us here four years ago, promising us food and good wages. My parents are very poor, so they agreed. But he never pays us. He starves us and beats us. He promised to send us home after a year but... I haven't seen my mother in four years," Aziz's face crumpled.

Mr. Mehra had joined them by now.

"This is Aziz," said Mrs. Mehra.

Mr. Mehra's eyes met hers in surprise. Mrs. Mehra told him Aziz's story.

"Can we take him home with us?" asked Divya.

"Wait," said their father. "Looks like this chap is illegally employing children. If we do anything now, he may get suspicious and try to hide, or even hurt them. We will go back and inform the authorities. It is not enough to take Aziz. All these children need help."

Mr. Mehra turned to Aziz and said kindly, "I promise I will get you out of here soon. You must have patience and do not talk of this to anyone."

Aziz nodded.

Malik, who had gone out to attend to a customer, returned. He looked suspicious when he saw them talking to Aziz. "You know him?" he asked.

"No," replied Mr. Mehra. "We liked the carpet he is weaving."

"Ah! Yes. A good worker. A bit of a dreamer, though."

"Well, thank you, Malikji, we learnt a lot about your factory today," said Mr. Mehra with ill-concealed sarcasm.

"What about the carpet madam liked?" asked Malik anxiously.

"In fact, we prefer the one the boy is making. We would like you to keep it for us," answered Mr. Mehra.

"Sure, sure," said Malik happily. "It will be ready in a week."

On the way back, Vicky asked, "What will we do to help Aziz?"

"I am going to inform the Labour Commissioner. He will take the necessary action," replied their father.

At home, the children could not stop worrying about Aziz. Everyday, they spoke to him through the carpet to cheer him up. Finally, one morning, their father showed them a big article on the front page of the newspaper. 'RAID ON LOCAL CARPET FACTORY: 20 CHILDREN FREED,' it said. There was a photograph of the children at the looms. Vicky and Divya scanned the faces anxiously.

"Where is Aziz?" wondered Divya.

"Here," said their mother.

The children swivelled around.

There, at the door, stood Aziz with a humble village couple.

"Meet my *Abba* (father) and *Ammi* (mother)," said Aziz. "They have come to take me home. Malik has been ordered to employ our fathers instead of us. At full wages. Now I can go to school!"

"Thanks to you children!" said his mother.

"No," said Divya, "thanks to Aziz's magic carpet!"

A Game of Tennis
Dipavali Debroy

Today was the day!

Ranesh, a student of Class VII, was impatient for school to end. The tennis match semi-finals at the Sports Complex were going to be held that day, right after school. He would go there directly from school as it was just a stone's throw away.

Ranesh was very keen on outdoor sports. He had missed getting into the finals of the local tennis tournament the previous year. He did not want to miss it again this time.

"But have you taken care of your history?" asked Vinay. "There is a revision test today."

"I forgot. In any case, I did not have the time. I was practising."

"Well then, beware of Sir H!" warned Vinay.

Sir H (for history) was an extremely strict teacher. He was a thin, young man with a tired look in his eyes. He had a sharp tongue and his students were not fond of him.

'Even if there is a test, I can't be bothered with history today,' thought Ranesh. 'Let this afternoon be over.'

Throughout the mathematics and physics classes, he sat wondering about how the afternoon would shape up. He hardly noticed when Sir H came into the classroom. Punit, his opponent for the match, was weak on his serves. "I must make use of that," he said to himself.

"What was the capital Harshvardhan ruled from?" Sir H asked. "You, Ranesh. And don't give me 'Kanauj'."

'What a serve!' Ranesh thought. 'How does one deal with it?'

"I assume the answer is beyond you. Well, it is Kanyakubjya. Kanauj is only a derivative. Okay. Which king of the Pratiharas took the title of *Adivaraha*, 'the first boar'?"

"Oh, what a bore," said someone from the back.

But Sir H's wrath fall on Ranesh. "Don't you have the answer to a single question? What were the years of King Bhoja's reign? Who was the first Pala king? Who was the second?" He shot one question after another at Ranesh. "Which dynasty came to rule the Pala kingdom in the end? Well, you find out. You jolly well find out after school."

"But, Sir..." Ranesh cried out.

"You will stay an extra hour after school and brush up your history. In the Staff Room. I will be there as well."

"I have got my tennis match today..." said Ranesh, agonized.

"Tennis, you say! Do you know the history of the word?"

Ranesh hung his head.

"It is a French word, *teniz*, which means 'hold it'. Before the game became popular in England, it was the French who played it. As one player served the ball to the other, he used to cry 'teniz' or 'hold it'. To English ears across the Channel, it sounded like 'tennis'. Did you know that?" Sir H stopped, out of breath.

"Now I do, Sir, thank you. Please let me off today," Ranesh said in his most wheedling tone.

"Nothing doing," said Sir H.

"Sir, please," pleaded Vinay. "He can't miss his match today!"

Sir H quelled him with a glance.

"It is important, Sir, this match," said Ranesh.

Sir H did not relent.

Ranesh wanted to slip out with the others right after school. But as soon as the last class was over, Sir H came up to his desk and collared him. Ranesh found himself sitting in a corner of the fast emptying Staff Room. "Read quietly about the kingdoms of the north," said Sir H. "I feel a bit tired. So don't be a pest."

Ranesh sat poring over his history textbooks while in the Sports Complex, on the green courts, the tennis match went on. The tears that came into his eyes made the dates hazy. Whenever he shuffled his feet, or squirmed in his seat, Sir H fixed him with a glare, even though he sat at the far end of the Staff Room. He sat with that book of his, delving deep into its pages and never looking up except when Ranesh made a movement.

'How I hate him,' thought Ranesh.

Suddenly Sir H gave a stifled cry and slumped on the table.

"Sir, what is wrong?" Ranesh jumped up from his seat and went over to him. How utterly tired Sir H looked. Ranesh shook him by the shoulder; the teacher did not respond.

'Let me get some water,' thought Ranesh and ran out of the Staff Room. From the cooler at the end of the corridor, he got some cold water and rushed back to the Staff Room. He splashed it over the drooping head.

Sir H blinked and mumbled something.

"Yes, Sir?"

"Sir Thomas Roe...Jehangir's Court...17..."

"Gosh, history dates even when unconscious!" said Ranesh.

As soon as he could open his eyes, Sir H said, "Thanks," and tried to get up.

He could not do so on his own. "My head hurts," he groaned.

Ranesh put his arm round Sir H's waist and hauled him up. Together, they tottered to the door and down the stairs to the main gate. Ranesh made the gatekeeper fetch an autorickshaw for him. With the gatekeeper's help, he got Sir H into the vehicle.

Sir H muttered an address and sank back upon the seat, eyes closed tiredly.

Ranesh knew he should not let him go by himself. He too got into the autorickshaw.

Luckily he had some money with him.

The address Sir H had given was of a shabby old house, clearly let out in portions. Once they were there, Sir H brought out a key from his pocket and fumbled with it. Ranesh had to unlock the door for him.

*   *   *

The room had hardly any furniture. Or eatables. Most of it was taken up by books. They were everywhere! Books, printed but unbound, reading material in large, brown envelopes, there were piles and piles of them. There were sheaves of note-paper as well, scattered all over the cement floor.

"Let me get you some food, Sir," said Ranesh as Sir H collapsed on his bed. He clattered down the stairs to a fast food shop on the opposite pavement.

"A hamburger and a pizza," he urged the man at the counter. "Quick!" He also got a cold drink and then charged up to Sir H.

Sir H tried to say something, but Ranesh shoved the piping hot pizza before his nose and he could not go on.

'He must have been starving,' thought Ranesh, as he watched Sir H gobble up the pizza and then fall upon the hamburger.

He offered the cold drink and Sir H drank it up in a long draught. "Th-thank you," he said gruffly, and fell muttering to himself, "must get into the Services this time. Must not fail again." His voice trailed off.

Ranesh settled him more comfortably on the bed, and left.

When he reached home, he found his parents worried and anxious that he had not turned up for the match he had been so keen on. Vinay and the other boys from his class who had

gone to watch the semi-finals told them how Sir H had detained
Ranesh at school. His parents had gone to the school to look
for him. By then the gates were locked and the gatekeeper too
had not been around. They came back home and found that
he still had not reached. Mummy was getting distraught, when
Ranesh, to their great relief, reached home.

Also anxious about Ranesh, Vinay dropped in. He told Ranesh
what he had known ever since Sir H had detained him. Rival
Punit had now made it to the finals. "All because of Sir H!"

Ranesh began to tell them about what had happened in the
Staff Room, and afterwards.

*   *   *

Next morning—a Sunday morning—Ranesh visited Sir H
again with home-cooked food and hot chocolate.

Ranesh found Sir H looking a little rested. His eyes still had
dark circles under them, but they lit up at the sight of Ranesh.

"Thanks for bringing me home yesterday!" He paused and
added, "I must have fainted yesterday because I was tired and
overworked. Now I feel bad about your tennis match. I was
pretty mean to you over that."

"Yes, Sir," agreed Ranesh at once.

"Tell me something. When I fainted, you had a chance of
running away to play the match. They usually wait a while
before giving the other fellow a walkover. Why didn't you take
that chance?"

"It just went out of my head then, the match," said Ranesh
simply.

Sir H's voice was husky when he spoke. "I know I can't quite
make it up to you. I will try. What about some tennis coaching
from me?" asked Sir H. "We could go over to the Sports Complex
everyday after school."

At Ranesh's stunned look, he laughed. "I was an inter-

24

university champion. I gave up my tennis because I thought it would eat into my study hours. You see, I am taking the Civil Service examinations for the third time."

He explained to Ranesh that it was a very tough competitive examination in which history was an important subject. People took this examination usually while working at some other job. If and when they cleared it, they became officers serving the country. It was a strain to most people because it meant studying and working side by side. It hardly left time for anything else.

"The last couple of years I have been poring over my books, and working to make both ends meet. I tried to save money by eating less and less and I tried to save time by studying more and more. When teaching you people at school, I was really preparing for my own exams. Especially in the case of history."

He went on, more to himself than to Ranesh, "The last two times I took the Civil Services exams, it was the history marks which pulled me down. I was determined not to let it happen again."

"I have gone to the other extreme," said Ranesh. "All play and no work. I shall put more into my studies from now on."

"And will you let me have another chance—with you?" asked Sir H. "I haven't had a very happy history with you, but..."

"I will forget about all that, Sir," said Ranesh. "You know how good I am at forgetting history."

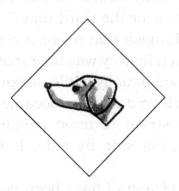

His Highness

Homagni Chaudhuri

It was a terrible morning. *Dadu* (grandfather) wanted to visit the library and consult some books. When he sat down for an early lunch, Mother told him that everything was closed for Puja. *Dadu* grumbled about lazy, inconsiderate people who enjoyed more and more holidays; they had no sense of duty. He was writing an article by invitation and was almost ready but he needed to check a few references. After a cup of coffee, *Dadu* cheered up and said, "We shall go for a walk."

Peppy, the dachshund, heard the good news, rushed out, and came back with his leash.

The two started out happily but soon came across a Puja *pandal* (marquee) blocking the road. Although there was a narrow passage by the side, *Dadu* did not want to squeeze through in an undignified manner. It would be better to take a small detour. He did not realize that with the Puja decorations on all sides, the neighbourhood looked quite different. He soon lost his bearings. Peppy tried to guide *Dadu* back but was firmly overruled.

Nini *Pishi* (paternal aunt) and Milu, out in the market-place

for some emergency purchase, found the two old gentlemen, tired and irritable, going round in circles. Nini *Pishi* asked suspiciously, "Are you lost?"

Dadu shook his head, gave a sad smile, and said, "You need to improve your manners and also your common sense. How can I be lost? I know all the lanes and bylanes. Peppy wanted a long walk."

Peppy gave a short, deep bark to indicate that things were under control, and with a gentle tug on the leash, persuaded *Dadu* to return home with the junior party.

Sarala, the cook, was on leave, away to her village home for two days. Mother had taken immense trouble and prepared an elaborate lunch to please everyone. For *Dadu*, who no longer ate meat or fish, there were the special, traditional, vegetarian dishes that needed lots of time and care to prepare. Father would, of course, have two types of fish, and there was meat for Peppy. Milu, as a growing girl, would have everything. Nini *Pishi* was a light eater and disliked being fussed over.

Sitting down for a holiday lunch was a well known drill. Sarala would call everyone, one by one, at least three times, before anyone moved for the long, leisurely meal. Peppy would be called each time *Dadu* was, and they would come in together. But today lunch was late and when Nini *Pishi* called, *Dadu*, not his usual self after the tiring morning walk, moved absent-mindedly to the dining table.

Dadu stretched out his hand towards a slice of lemon when he noticed that his loyal companion of fourteen years was not by his side. "Where is Peppy?" he asked in a shocked and surprised voice.

"My goodness," exclaimed Nini *Pishi*. "I forgot to call His Highness. This has been a bad day. Milu, be a good girl, and bring him along."

"Be careful," said Father.

Everyone knew that when Peppy was angry, he retreated to

his blanket which was under *Dadu*'s bed, and, except *Dadu*, no one was allowed to come anywhere near. Peppy knew that at his age he could not possibly guard the entire house, but he would certainly defend the place where *Dadu* and he had their beds. A few days earlier, when Father, rather than walk through the dark, crowded passageway, took a short cut through *Dadu*'s room late at night, he had strayed near the bed and was smartly nipped in the ankle.

From a safe distance, Milu peered under the bed. She saw Peppy's eyes glowing red like burning coals, and a low growl left no doubt that he was very angry.

And indeed Peppy was. The fourteen-year-old dog shook and quivered with irritation. How dare the others, not *Dadu* of course, forget to call him for lunch. They had actually started eating before *Dadu* could speak up. He, Peppy Chaudhuri, the second senior member of the family, had been ignored! How dare they, overgrown puppies all of them!

Father, Mother and Nini *Pishi* were merely Biku, Lina and Nini to him. And Milu had hardly cut her milk teeth. When Peppy, at five, was a responsible adult, he used to take two-year-old Milu out for short walks in front of the house. He would drag her along the footpath and keep her safe. Now though Milu, at eleven, was much bigger, Peppy still had a soft spot for her and sometimes, as a special treat, allowed the youngest to pull him around.

When he had first come in as a puppy, he used to scatter food around, and was fed in the veranda. He was a neat eater now and, long ago, his bowl had been shifted inside; *Dadu* wanted it that way. Peppy deserved his place in the dining room. He never made a mess. He stopped when *Dadu* did, and if *Dadu* took longer, he drank more water and licked his bowl clean. But for no reason whatsoever, these rude youngsters, who had no manners and argued noisily at the table, had insulted him. He growled again.

Surprised and a little frightened, Milu slowly returned to the dining room, and said, "Peppy is under the bed and is very very angry."

"A crank in his old age," said Nini *Pishi*. "No manners at all. Anyway, when he is hungry enough, he will have to come out."

"Nini, you are the one who was rude," objected *Dadu*. "Peppy is a gentleman and doesn't lose his temper unless provoked."

Nini *Pishi* taught mathematics in a college and believed in order and method. Tantrums were to be ignored. Mother was upset. All the dishes had turned out well but a member of the family was refusing to eat. She looked at Father, and said, "Do something."

"Oh, all right," said Father. "I will pull him out." As he got up, Mother went along with him.

Peppy heard. He knew what to do if anyone pulled him, and he knew that they also knew. He was a pure bred Dachshund, killer of a thousand vermin and, in his own territory, he was not frightened of anyone. However, he would give fair warning. He growled again.

Mother and Father dropped the idea and came back. *Dadu* said regretfully, "If it hadn't been for my arthritis, I would have dragged him out."

Peppy heard. He did not move. The juniors had to be punished. He was not one of the beggarly street dogs. He could smell the meat in his bowl, tasty mutton, the best, soft pieces because of his old teeth but he would not eat, he would starve.

Peppy was *Dadu*'s companion. The two constituted the senior citizens' club, one, a staunch vegetarian, and the other, a strict non-vegetarian. Everyone in the neighbourhood respected them. When they walked out, children wished them and other dogs gave way.

When he had been brought to the house, hardly anyone knew about dachshunds. The street dogs made rude noises and impertinent children muttered about Peppy being a rat catcher, not a proper dog. His smart bearing impressed everyone and word spread about his aristocratic ancestry. Peppy lived up to his image, that was a duty he owed to *Dadu*, the family and himself. Now it seemed the family did not care for him, not even Nini or Milu. *Dadu* and he were being ignored. He would teach them. He would starve; he would not beg.

Peppy did not come out for tea . He did not go for his evening walk, not even when *Dadu* called him again and again. When the family sat down for dinner, everyone was in a bad mood. Peppy was still under the bed. Nini *Pishi* remembered his last two-day hunger strike and shivered. Tomorrow would be *Ashtami,* the day for special feasting. Peppy could not be allowed to sulk. Nini *Pishi* shrugged, and opened the fridge.

Peppy smelt the liver and knew it was going to be difficult. Nini was a great favourite of his. She tickled him behind the ears and spoilt him silly with banned *rosogollas* (a sweetmeat), two at a time. Now he was going to be bribed. Peppy sighed.

Sure enough. Nini's face appeared under the bed, and her hand held out a large piece of liver. Peppy drooled. Then he remembered. Dachshunds could not be bribed. Dignity before diet. He growled.

Nini *Pishi* crawled in farther. The smell and the sight of the large piece of liver was too much. Peppy could not check his drooling. Extreme measures were called for. Peppy charged out, nipped Nini *Pishi's* hand, and rushed away.

Milu heard Nini *Pishi* crying, "Ouch," and then a happy, "Woof" as Peppy, tail wagging, came into the dining room.

"Hurrah!" said Milu.

When Nini *Pishi*, after washing the bite, returned to the dining table, Peppy went out, brought back the liver piece and placed it in his bowl. He had his manners, no gorging. And he would forgive Nini. He stood up on two legs, licked her, and then barked to indicate that everything was all right. Life was not so bad, even though sometimes you had to put up a good fight.

Twin Trouble
Agila Girirajkumar

The house was very quiet except for the occasional sob. Ranjan had been whipped by his father because his quarterly examination report said, "Promotion doubtful!"

Father was in his room, looking grim. Ranjan was lying on the ground, head in his mother's lap, crying. And Ravi was hungry—for food and for praise. He looked at his own report card. It read, "Brilliant! Keep it up!"

He had come first in his class. Did anybody care? They had noticed that Ranjan had failed in three subjects, had they not?

Ravi decided he needed some attention. He went to his father and said, "*Appa*, my report!"

His father read it through, patted his shoulder and said, "Very good!"

'Is that all?' wondered Ravi.

Then his father added, "Show this to that fool, your brother."

"What about me, *Appa*?" Ravi wanted to cry. "*Me*, by *myself*? Are you not proud of *me*?" But he had no faith in his parents' ability to understand his feelings. He remained silent. He ached to hear words of genuine praise from his parents. They did not come. He went to his mother. "*Amma,* I am hungry!"

She did not even look at him. "Can't you see everything is on the table? Eat what you want!" she exclaimed irritably.

Glumly, Ravi surveyed the food. Potatoes, finely cubed and fried—the way Ranjan liked it! Eggs hard boiled—the way Ranjan liked it! Ravi liked eggs scrambled and potatoes in a curry. Why did *Amma* not make that nowadays? Why was everything the way Ranjan wanted it? He did not deserve it!

A sudden rage possessed Ravi. He emptied the bowl of potatoes on to his plate and, like it or not, he finished it! Then he waited for the reaction.

When his mother finally coaxed Ranjan to the table, she found the bowl empty. She came storming at Ravi. "Don't you have any sense? What will Ranjan eat now?"

His brother's name grated on Ravi's nerves! He yelled back, "Let him eat whatever there is! Let him starve! Then he will learn not to fail!"

His mother's anger exploded. "I don't need your help to punish Ranjan," she screamed at him. "With *Appa* beating him and you starving him, what will he do?" she raged. She whirled out of the house to buy some more potatoes.

Ravi glared at Ranjan. 'Stupid, puny fellow! When I am studying, he goes on playing. And Amma runs behind him begging him not to tire himself saying, "Drink milk", "Drink juice".' His thoughts ran on, 'When I ask her for the smallest help, she says, "Can't you do it yourself? I can't run behind both of you!" How can she forget she is my mother too! She keeps ignoring me for Ranjan! He causes me no end of trouble! I hate him!'

Ravi's unhappiness over his parents' attitude kept growing. He did not keep up his usual standard in the half-yearly examinations. His teachers were displeased with his tenth rank; Ravi was secretly thrilled. Now *Appa* and *Amma* would beg him and coax him to study! He was a little worried *Appa* might whip him. Even then, *Amma* would make his favourite dish and beg him to eat!

He handed over his report card and waited in pleasurable anticipation, Alas! No storm broke over his head! His parents were merely annoyed with him. "Just when we were happy that Ranjan passed in all subjects, you bring a report like this! Can't we ever be happy about both of you?"

Ranjan again! Ravi gnashed his teeth. "I have still got better marks than Ranjan," he returned sulkily.

"Stop comparing," ordered his father.

By now Ravi was very angry. He thought of various ways to gain his parents' attention. Finally he decided, 'I will fail. Like Ranjan, I will fail, once. The next time I shall pass. Then they will hug me and praise me!'

Ravi found this resolution difficult to carry out. He loved to study. He could not be inattentive in class even if he wanted to. He could never go to school without doing his homework.

However, he badly wanted the kind of love his parents showered on Ranjan. The only way to that seemed to be to fail! Could he? Caught in this internal conflict, Ravi became more and more miserable each day.

His parents had fallen into the habit of thinking that Ravi would take care of himself. They concentrated on the weaker Ranjan. So involved were they in Ranjan's progress that they were completely unaware that Ravi hungered for their attention.

The mid-term tests had begun. Ravi had studied entirely against his will. He still wanted to fail.

He glanced down at the mathematics question paper. He knew everything! The conflict raged within him! How could he possibly do even one sum wrong? If he did well, his parents would forget he even existed!

His eyes filled with tears. Ashamed, he wiped them away. More tears came! A sob escaped his lips. Before he even realized it, he was crying uncontrollably.

His mathematics teacher came up to him, "Ravi, what is the matter with you? Are you sick?"

Ravi could not stop crying even to answer. He had borne his pain privately for too long.

The rest of the class stared at the sight of the teacher's favourite pupil crying hard instead of writing steadily.

The teacher sent the sobbing child to the Headmaster.

The Headmaster asked Ravi to drink some water. When Ravi had calmed down, he asked, "Were you crying because you didn't know the answers?"

Ravi's lips quivered again. 'I know everything,' he wanted to say. 'But I must not write!'

'Why not?' he would be asked.

Ravi was silent. How did one explain? Even if one did, would the Headmaster understand?

The mathematics teacher praised Ravi to the Headmaster in no uncertain terms.

Puzzled, the Headmaster called Ravi's father to his office.

Thinking it was Ranjan in trouble, *Appa* dashed to the school in record time. He could not believe his eyes when he saw Ravi in the Headmaster's room.

"Ravi! What have *you* done?"

Ravi's feelings were threatening to choke him again. He turned his head away!

The Headmaster said, "Your son started crying in class instead of doing his test. Do you know what the problem is?"

Appa was startled! "He is a very good boy, Sir! He studies without coaxing. We never worry about him..."

Suddenly Ravi exploded, "I want you to worry me. Whenever Ranjan fails, you love him better. I thought you will love me too if I fail. Otherwise you don't care about me! You don't love me! You don't want me! That is why I wanted to fail! How can I fail? I know everything!"

Appalled, *Appa* stared at him.

The Headmaster looked at *Appa* gravely. "That is a very heavy burden for a small boy to carry at this age. Each individual child is precious. Why have you given this child the impression that you are more loving to the other?"

It took *Appa* a minute to speak. Then he said, with difficulty, "Sir, Ravi and Ranjan are twins. Right from birth, Ranjan has been very weak. Even now he is small for his age. His resistance is very low. He catches every illness possible. With him, it is always serious. That is why we are so protective towards him. That is why we have fallen into the habit of coddling him, while taking Ravi for granted. You see, we keep wishing he were more like Ravi! Sometimes I get so frustrated that Ranjan is not like Ravi; I lose my temper and whip him!"

"That is very wrong," stated the Headmaster firmly.

"It won't happen again. In fact, none of this will happen again," promised *Appa*.

While the adults were talking, Ravi was remembering the time, six months ago, when Ranjan had been sick. His parents had spent every available minute by his bedside, besides cancelling their holiday trip. That was when Ravi's resentment had really begun. He had raged, "Twins are supposed to be soulmates. Ranjan is a soul-destroyer. He has taken my parents' love away from me. He has never been my friend!"

Thinking back, Ravi regretted his anger. '*Amma* and *Appa* were taking care of Ranjan so that he would be with me always,' he thought. 'How could I have been so thoughtless? I should have been a good friend to Ranjan. When he was sick, I could have cheered him up!' He tried to imagine a life without Ranjan. Utter black desolation stared him in the face.

Aghast, he exclaimed, "Oh! no!"

His father and the Headmaster looked enquiringly at him.

"*Appa*," said Ravi hesitantly, "I am sorry I have been selfish. From now on I will help you to take care of Ranjan."

His father's face glowed with happiness and relief that the

crisis that had threatened to destroy all peace at home, had passed without causing much damage.

Ravi turned to the Headmaster and said, "Sir, from next year, could you please put both of us in the same section? Then I can help Ranjan in his studies."

The Headmaster nodded but warned, "Don't neglect your studies. That is also important. I shall arrange for you to take this exam another day."

Thanking him, father and son walked out with light steps. The Headmaster smiled in satisfaction.

Grandad's Happy Hour

Neela Subramaniam

Vivek dawdled on his way home from school. He was late as he had stayed back to watch a cricket match.

He knew that his mother would be quite frantic with worry, he was sure that she would scold him for not having sent word through his friends when he knew he was going to be late. He was in for an unexpected surprise.

A crowd of people—mostly women and children—had collected at the entrance of the staircase of the apartment complex where he lived. He wondered what had happened. Vivek's eyes fell on his mother. She was wiping her eyes with the end of her saree. He was alarmed. What had happened, he wondered uneasily as he elbowed his way to her side.

"Why are you crying, *Amma?*" he asked anxiously. He felt guilty now.

"Oh, Vivek! I am so glad to see you!" A smile of relief spread across her face.

"Take it easy, *Amma!* Just tell me what happened," Vivek murmured soothingly. He was relieved to note that she had overlooked his latecoming in her pleasure at seeing him.

"I had come downstairs to check the letter-box and had left
the front door of our flat open. But the wind slammed it shut.
It is locked now," Mrs. Srinivasan explained. "I rang the bell
many times. As your Grandad is quite deaf, it is probable that
he didn't hear anything!"

"*Amma*, you could have opened the door with the key which
you usually have!" Vivek pointed out logically.

Mrs. Srinivasan looked abashed.

"I left it in the bathroom when I went to wash my face."

"Oh! You can't contact *Appa* as he will be back from Delhi
only tomorrow," Vivek whistled. "Tell me, *Amma*, how long has
this been going on?"

"For about half an hour. I am worried because Grandad may
have fallen asleep. He was relaxing with a book when I last
saw him," his mother looked more and more worried.

Vivek was silent for a moment. He searched for a face in the
crowd and turned to his mother.

"*Amma*, where is the watchman?" he demanded.

"It is his afternoon off," Mrs. Srinivasan reminded her son.

Vivek put down his schoolbag and looked around. A branch
of the mango tree which grew in the compound of the house
next door almost reached the window of their drawing and
dining room.

"I shall climb up and see what Grandad's doing. Perhaps I
will be able to attract his attention and make him open the
door." Vivek kicked off his shoes.

The women from the other flats shouted encouragingly as
Vivek shinned up the mango tree and crawled along the branch.

"That is enough, Vivek! Don't go any farther or you will fall!"
his mother shouted anxiously. "Now, tell me, can you see your
grandad? What is he doing?"

"No, there is no sign of him. Perhaps he is napping in the
bedroom. I shall wait for some time," Vivek called back and
settled down as comfortably as he could.

Feeling hungry, he felt in his pocket for the chocolate bar he had bought on his way home. Vivek peeled away the wrapper and began eating.

His jaws ceased working when the familiar figure of his Grandad came into view. To Vivek's surprise, the old man went to the front door and made sure that it was locked. Then, he rubbed his hands and smiled broadly as he disappeared into the kitchen.

"What is he doing?" Vivek was mystified. He waited.

His Grandad reappeared a few minutes later. He held a plate heaped with sweets. Vivek stifled a grin. Grandad was helping himself to the sweets his mother had been making for his birthday party to be held the following evening.

The doctor had forbidden Grandad from eating sweets for some months as his blood sugar count was a little high and had to be controlled. But here he was gobbling sweets on the sly! Talk of the mouse playing when the cat is away! Vivek chortled with silent glee. He found it difficult to school his features into solemnity when he was vividly aware that his every move was being watched by the crowd below.

Vivek found himself strangely unable to tell his mother that he had seen his grandad. He just could not give Grandad away.

He remembered the numerous occasions when the old man had been his companion and staunch ally in escapades which had invited parental wrath... Like the time when Vivek and his parents had gone to Grandad's ancestral home years ago. Vivek and Grandad had returned home drenched one day. His mother had scolded Vivek. Grandad had intervened to inform his daughter that he was really to blame as he had wanted to show Vivek his secret hiding-place near the river...

Another time, Vivek had confided to his grandad, who lived with them now after Grandma passed away and the ancestral home was sold, that he had done poorly in mathematics in his half-yearly exams.

"I know *Appa* and *Amma* will raise the roof! I am very scared," Vivek remembered confessing to Grandad.

"Don't worry, I will see to it!" Grandad had assured the nervous boy.

After supper, he had called his daughter and son-in-law and told them that he was feeling bored and intended supervising Vivek's homework.

"He is very weak in maths. I shall see to it that he scores full marks in his finals. I won't be surprised if he has secured low marks in maths this time!" Grandad had ended.

It was the cue for Vivek to produce his report card. He was thankful that Grandad had paved the way with his warning about his performance in maths. His parents simply told him to pull up his socks and do better next time!

'Let him enjoy himself now!' Vivek thought defiantly. He pretended that he had not seen anything to report to his mother and continued eating his chocolate. As Vivek watched, Grandad's face took on an ecstatic expression when he lifted the sugar-crusted *burfi* (a sweetmeat) and savoured its rich aroma before eating it very slowly to relish every bite!

Suddenly Grandad's eyes fell on Vivek peering in at the window. A look of utter horror spread across his face. He raised a finger to his lips for silence. Vivek nodded his head slightly to reassure Grandad when he noted the wistful, pleading look in his eyes. His own mouth watered as Grandad resumed eating the sweets.

Then Grandad came near the window and whispered, "I will go and wash the plate and clean up the place before your mother catches me. He...hhheee! She won't smell a rat as I have taken care to remove the sweets from the bottom of the containers! Give me a few more minutes, please, Vivek!"

"Vivek! Have you seen Grandad?" his mother called.

"Nooo...yes! He is coming into the room now. I shall try to attract his attention," Vivek said when he saw Grandad emerging from the kitchen wiping his hands. He broke off some twigs from the branch he sat on. As Grandad watched smilingly, Vivek flung them in one by one and pretended that none had caught Grandad's eye. Then Vivek plucked a small, green mango and took careful aim.

"There! Grandad has seen me! I shall make him realize that the front door is locked and that we want him to open it." Vivek waved his arms and made suitable actions to tell the old man what he wanted.

Grandad watched Vivek's performance with a huge grin on his face. Then he relented and went across the room to open the front door.

Mrs. Srinivasan ran upstairs quickly and was relieved to see her father who told her that he had been enjoying himself thinking of Vivek's birthday party!

"I am glad nothing else happened!" Mrs. Srinivasan exclaimed.

Vivek heard his Grandad's explanation with a quiet smile.

"So am I. We can all happily share the delights of my party, Grandad!" he said.

At his party, Vivek offered the first slice of the birthday cake to Grandad with a small wink.

"This is specially for you, Grandad! Just a small piece of my cake—you must eat it. I won't take 'No' for an answer!" Vivek laughed.

"Thank you, Vivek! May God bless you for your kind heart!" Grandad replied solemnly with a tiny wink.

All the same, Vivek was heartily relieved to note that Grandad suffered from no ill-effects after his stolen treat.

The following day, Grandad pointed to a verse in a book of quotations he was reading:

"One crowded hour of glorious life
Is worth an age without a name..."

Yes, it was a crowded hour of glorious life for Grandad!

The House That Walked
Sarojine Chopra

Thakur Ram Hari Singh stood at the edge of the open field.
Rubble, dust and weeds stretched before him. Here and there
was a recognizable piece of broken brick. Nothing else was
familiar in the mess in front of his eyes. He decided to walk
around this vast field. He needed to bring back the memory of
what it once had been.

As he walked forward he stumbled upon an old pit. Here had
stood the towering mango tree of his childhood capers. How
many times had he hidden there until the wrath of one or the
other parent had blown over. Farther down, more familiar places
jogged his memory. Sometimes the roots of trees and, here
and there, an old stump stood in sad splendour. Nothing else.

He gave up mid-way. What was the use? His walk would not
bring anything back to its former self. The opposite might
happen; he could be overwhelmed by sadness, he might even
weep with sorrow and frustration. He had to think of the correct
words with which to tell his family what he had seen. Action
was needed, not just this terrible turmoil of feelings. What action
could he take—against whom? Where would he need to begin?

45

He retraced his steps. Sadly, he said the words to himself. Gently at first, then with increasing firmness. "Yes, the house has walked away...The house has walked...aw...ay." He shook himself as if out of a bad dream. "It is true, it is not there."

It had begun a full two decades earlier. He, the scion of the Thakur family, had inherited the entire estate. The Thakurs were the first family of Balliat. A region rich and fertile, it yielded crops in regular measure. The crops turned to money for the Thakurs. The money turned to solid gold. That, in turn, was put in strong boxes of the large house. Many a bounty of the land also accompanied the money. Bags full of raw mangoes, baskets full of ripe oranges and as for the vegetables, there were always heaps and heaps. Nearly roomfuls.

The house itself had no architectural style. It was vast and big. Added to when more rooms were needed. A son being born, a wedding taking place and such like were the reasons for additions. The logical placement of these was never given a thought. Some rooms were, therefore, large, others were poky and airless. In the end, the place resembled a castle with turrets, balconies, open courtyards, parapets and any feature which was the then owner's fancy. The inside too had reflected the richness of expensive tastes.

Surrounding the house were many trees. Nearly every occasion of celebration was an excuse to plant a new tree. As expected, they too were not planted in neat and orderly rows. It was rather a jungle effect. The trees teemed with life. Not only birds of several hues but a number of small animals sheltered there. Naughty children would clamber over the walls on sleepy afternoons to do what naughty children do the world over. The garden was as active a place as the large and sprawling house it belonged with.

Gradually the children of the household grew up. Daughters were married off to other households of vast spreads. The only son was sent to expensive schools and colleges. Summers were spent in new hill stations and winters in smart towns. The house stood empty for weeks on end.

When Ram Hari had grown up he had managed to get a very good job in far-off Calcutta. He returned to Balliat less frequently. Whenever he needed money he was used to asking for it. Now that he was the head of the estate, he had to fend for it himself. He was not trained to work out the incomes from the lands of his forefathers. He did the easier thing. He would agree to sell a small piece of the fertile land. He had acquired a passion for fast cars. Travel was his next desire. Both these needed a large flow of cash. The lands were sold even more quickly. He came to be called *'Thakur Sahib do paise ki zamin bechne wale'* (the Thakur Sahib who sells land for a song).

All this suited Ram Hari's lifestyle. He did not spare a thought for his dwindling estate. After some time, the only thing left in his possession was the house, 'Thakur Niwas'. He stopped short of selling it out of a vague consideration that it would serve him as a country place. He could entertain special guests there.

At this point, a local, petty official of Balliat came to meet him. His name was Seva Singh. Round, his hair groomed with a strong smelling oil, he was not welcomed at the beautiful Calcutta home of Ram Hari. He was prepared to wait. He did not notice the looks of disdain that were directed at him. He waited patiently. He had a proposal, he said. He wanted to rent the Niwas. Quickly he named a good figure before the Thakur could refuse him. A deal was struck, advance money was produced. The sight of the cash was what made Ram Hari decide. The lowly Seva Singh was on his way out.

The money was converted into a vacation for the family. Ram Hari was even more delighted when the next instalment of rent arrived in time by a money order. Others followed with pleasing regularity. No demands were made for repairs or deductions of any sort.

'Good old fellow,' thought Ram Hari.

However, one month the money order did not come. It was hardly noticed. A second month went by the same way, followed by a third and a fourth. Then several more. Between his many preoccupations Ram Hari decided to send a polite letter to Seva Singh. He suggested that the account be brought up to date.

Nothing happened.

Another letter. The language was less flowery and more to the point.

There was no reply.

A registered letter, a registered A.D.

No response.

The Thakur's wife began to nag. Since his lifestyle only equipped him to deal with office pressures, the nagging was painful to bear. He was persuaded to take definite action.

Still a few years were to pass before gearing up.

At last he was on his way to Balliat with anger in his heart. He would bring Seva Singh down a peg or two. If need be, he would get the house vacated. If it was inconvenient—too bad, he had asked for it.

Ram Hari got off at the wayside station. He hired a tonga and, with a sharp command, ordered the driver to proceed to Balliat. The man was about to bargain for the price. He thought that the city slicker would pay a whole five rupees. On arrival at Balliat, Ram Hari put on his best Thakur air and said, "Thakur Niwas *chalo* (drive to Thakur Niwas)."

He drew his first blank here. The young driver had not heard the name. Ram Hari had to jog his own memory about the turnings yet he said with confidence, "Seva Singh *ka ghar* (Seva Singh's house)."

"Seva Singh does not live here any more."

"What!"

"Yes, sahib, he left when my sister got married. When was that? Let us see...yes, when Hoshiar Singh had a good crop."

"Quiet, quiet," stammered the Thakur. "Where has Seva Singh

gone? How could he...have left...he sent me...!" The rest of the sentence trailed away in a jumble of thought.

The tonga driver asked his puzzled fare, "Where next?"

"To the place where Seva Singh lived. To the house, whatever it is called."

"House, sahib, house...no...no...house!"

"Take me there," shouted the Thakur.

Approaching the land, Ram Hari leapt out of the tonga, throwing a handful of money at the tonga driver in his hurry to get off.

He raced to the place where Thakur Niwas had once stood. He was met by dust and rubble, tree stumps and a lonely wind sweeping over the barrenness.

Ram Hari raced back to habitation. He sought out the petty officials, who were of no help at all. He dug up a few old men smoking their endless hookahs on sun-drenched squares.

In amazement he listened to a narration of strange events. Years earlier Seva Singh returned to Balliat. He announced that he had bought the house from Thakurji. He boasted a bit, but generally kept to himself.

The *Patwari* who wondered that the transaction had not been indicated to him, was glibly told that Thakurji would come himself to register the deed. The *Patwari,* used to the rich man's ways, left the matter pending in his mind. Gradually it was forgotten. Nothing further was done.

A short while after this, Seva Singh began to remove the furniture and other things that were movable to flea markets. The Calcutta end was being taken care of all this time. When the house was shorn and empty, Seva Singh announced that he was building an estate not very far away. The same locals who, years earlier, had raised the walls and laid the floors of Thakur Niwas were now engaged to dismantle them.

Slowly, carved doors and windows found new homes. Chandeliers were hung in other rich homes. Less fancy fittings were dismantled. Marble floors were lifted, trellised **screens** and tiled paths followed. Bricks of good quality were sent in one direction, the broken ones in another. Whole walls disappeared. The shell was reduced to the foundations. These too were dug lest a treasure or two lay there. Now nothing, nothing remained.

Seva Singh had helped himself to what everyone thought was rightfully his.

A point was reached when it was safe to stop the Calcutta payments. The rest was history.

Ram Hari tried in vain to follow tracts. Seva Singh had well guessed the quality of the pursuit that might follow. It came to an end long before it had really begun.

No doubt in some quiet street of a quiet town, an old chandelier lights up Seva Singh's pate while he reclines on the Thakur's favourite chair thinking of the next *seva* (service) to the world.

Odd One In

Tithi Tavora

"How was the first day of school?" asked Mother as Rima sat down for dinner.

"Okay," Rima shrugged. "No lessons. Just settling in."

"Any new girls in your class?" enquired her father, Mr. Sen.

"Only one—Malti—and she is funny," grimaced Rima as she helped herself to the salad.

"Why do you say that?" asked Mr. Sen.

"She can't speak much English. She has come from another State," sniffed Rima, naming one at the other end of the country.

"Oh! Children from that State are supposed to be clever. They are specially good at maths," said Mr. Sen quietly.

"Well, this one does not seem smart at all. Oily hair, *bindi* (dot marked on forehead) and all. 'Gud marning, Teeechurr'," mimicked Rima.

Her parents exchanged glances. Rima was their only child. They doted on her. But she could be insufferable at times.

"I do hope you and your friends will not make things too difficult for Malti," sighed Mr. Sen as he rose from the table.

Rima and her gang had decided to do just that.

Next morning, the minute Malti entered the class, they all chorused, "Gud marning!"

Poor Malti. She did not realize that they were making fun of her. She beamed back at them and replied, "Gud marning!"

Shahnaz giggled. "Why do you put so much oil on your hair?" she asked rudely.

Malti looked offended but did not reply.

"And the skirt—so-o l-o-o-n-g," said Clare cattily.

Malti flushed. She was about to say something when Teacher entered. As the class progressed, everyone was surprised to see Malti raise her hand whenever Teacher asked a question.

"Yes, Malti, you answer," said Teacher.

Malti answered correctly and Teacher nodded in appreciation.

When Rima recounted this at home, her mother said, "Sounds like a clever girl."

"What is the use?" said Rima uncharitably. "Her English is so atrocious."

"The same may be said of your Hindi," countered Mr. Sen sharply. He was getting quite sick of Rima's attitude.

Even Mrs. Sen did not like it. That night Rima's parents discussed the matter.

"We put Rima into a good school to make her smart and confident. I am afraid she is turning into quite a little snob!" said Mr. Sen sadly.

The following Saturday was the Inter-House singing competition. Rima, who was participating in the English song category, was surprised to see Malti's name in the list of participants for the Hindi song category. "Oily plaits sings also," she said snidely to Clare.

"Croaks, you mean," giggled Clare.

They were to be proved wrong.

Malti sang beautifully. She had a melodious and well-trained voice. Rima and her gang had decided to jeer when Malti sang, but there was such absolute silence, they did not dare to. They

were sure to get caught. When Malti finished, the Principal was the first one to start clapping, followed by the teachers and students.

No one was surprised when Malti won the first prize. Rima did come first in her category; somehow, she felt no joy.

As the term progressed, it was abundantly clear to all that Malti was a bright child. She was quiet, studious and intelligent. She fared well in sports as well as in studies. Her forte was mathematics. Her simple appearance belied a sharp and nimble brain. Slowly, many of the girls began seeking her help in mathematics. Help which she readily and cheerfully gave. The teachers had liked the respectful, intelligent girl from the beginning. Now girls from the class also befriended her.

Not Rima and her clique though. They stubbornly disliked Malti. They were a stylish lot and nothing that Malti did could alter the fact that she was not their type. They never lost a chance to poke fun at her, particularly her English.

Malti felt bad about their behaviour. One day, she was on the verge of tears when Rima mocked at her mercilessly because she said "aks" instead of "ask".

Her voice trembling, Malti said, "I know my English is weak. Yours is good. Please, will you help me to improve it?"

"I won't be able to help you, my dear," replied Rima with an exaggerated accent. "Speaking proper English isn't easy for you countrified types!"

Malti's face turned red. She wanted to retort but could not find the right words. She burst into tears and ran off.

"That was horrid, Rima," said Shahnaz.

"Yes," agreed Neha and Clare roundly.

Rima was shocked. Her own friends had turned against her! She walked off in a huff.

Mrs. Sen found her subdued over lunch but decided not to ask anything. Rima knew that she had behaved very badly. She was too proud to admit it—even to herself.

She woke up with a heavy head the next day. She put it down to having had little sleep the previous night. Her mother, however, thought otherwise.

"You look flushed, Rima. Aren't you feeling well?" she enquired, touching Rima's forehead. "My goodness! You have fever! Get back into bed. No going to school today," she ordered.

Rima was only too glad. She felt so weak. She felt no better the next day. The doctor advised her to remain in bed for a whole week.

Rima was upset. The term tests would start the following Monday. Missing this week of school before the examinations would be a big handicap. Important questions and answers would be discussed in class. She would miss it all!

"Oh! Mummy! What will I do?" she wailed.

"Try to study as much as you can on your own. When your friends come, you can ask them what they were taught in class," replied her mother.

None of Rima's friends came to visit her.

Rima's mother was furious. "What fair-weather friends," she said to her husband. "At least they could have dropped in to see how Rima was."

To console Rima she said, "It is understandable. They must be busy studying for the tests."

"They could have called," complained Rima.

Mrs. Sen had no answer to that.

That afternoon, Rima had visitors. She was astonished when her mother led them into the room. It was Malti and a pretty, graceful lady, evidently her mother, because Malti resembled her quite a lot.

"Hello, Rima! I heard you were sick. How are you feeling now?" Malti asked.

Rima was so dumbfounded that she could not reply. She was overcome with gratitude, guilt, shame, and astonishment.

Mrs. Sen watched Rima closely. She felt some satisfaction at her daughter's discomfiture. 'Good!' she thought to herself. 'Our Rima is realizing that there is more to friends than stylish clothes and smart talk.'

Seeing that Rima was quiet, Malti's mother said, "You must be worried about having missed school during revision week. Don't worry. Malti can help you."

"Of course!" agreed Malti. "And you can help me with English."

Rima hung her head in shame. "Thank you, Malti, you are very kind." She got up and gave Malti a hug. "I am sorry I was so mean to you, Malti," she whispered.

"Forget it. I already have," said Malti, squeezing Rima's hand.

Both the mothers exchanged glances and smiled.

Nani's *Football Match*

Sudarshan Kumar Bhatia

"*Dada* (paternal grandfather), tell me a story," said Sonu.

For Ram Vilas, it was a routine every evening. Today he was pensive. His *Nani* (maternal grandmother) had died on April 6, 1955. A year later, on the same day, his *Nana* (maternal grandfather) too expired. Was it a coincidence that it was again the same day in April?

"*Dada*, have you gone to sleep? Wake up and tell me a story," Sonu repeated.

"Yes, Sonu, today I will tell you a story which is both real and interesting. It is about my *Nani*." Thus, Ram Vilas began.

"*Nani* was somewhat short—an inch or two below five feet. Her hair was more grey than black. Her face was chiselled, square, very fair, with two bright eyes. She had strong hands. The mother of five sons and two daughters who were all married, *Nani* held authority over her children and their twenty-odd children. Being the Zamindar's wife, and in her own right, she was the first lady of the village of 200 houses.

"*Nana* was six feet tall. He was bald but had a heavy, white moustache. In his younger days *Nana* had been a keen wrestler who usually felled all his rivals. *Nana* was a rich *sahukar* (banker) and the owner of 500 acres of land with orchards and rich, crop-yielding fields spread on all sides of the village. *Nana* was respected for his wisdom and feared for his strength."

"*Dada,* was your *Nani* more beautiful than my *Dadi* (paternal grandmother)? Was your *Nana* stronger than you?" interjected Sonu.

Ram Vilas laughed at his grandson's query and said, "Yes, Sonu, my *Nana* was very, very strong but your *Dadi* is more beautiful than my *Nani*. My *Nani* was wise. Let me tell you what happened in my grandparents' house," and, nostalgically, continued his narration.

"Sonu, our village was about 200 miles from Lahore, now in Pakistan. The place was a haven for us for the 15 days when our school closed for Dussehra and Diwali. My mother, Deepa, my sister, and I travelled by Karachi Mail to reach Multan by late afternoon. *Nana's* tonga carried us from the railway station to Sultanpur, our village.

"On the outskirts of the village was a big pond, at one end of which was a peepul tree. The entire village waited there for us, the children shouting, 'Ramu *aa gaya* (Ramu has come), Ramu *aa gaya.*' The elders embraced my mother and blessed her, '*Jeeti raho, beti* (May you live long, daughter). Welcome home. You must visit us one day.' Beyond the peepul were two houses owned by *Nana's* two brothers. My mother's uncles and their wives would bless my mother, and kiss us with affection. The finale was at *Nani's haveli* (mansion), the biggest pucca house in Sultanpur. *Nani* would welcome us each with a kiss on our foreheads, hold her daughter and say, 'Vidya, I miss you all the time.' Then it was our turn, 'Ramu, *jeete raho*. Deepa, love, how are you?' Oh, in those moments *Nani* was the kindest fairy on earth!"

"*Dada,* hurry up, please. Tell me the real story now," Sonu was growing impatient.

Ram Vilas realized that he had become emotional. "Don't be impatient," he told his grandson. "I must tell you everything in detail and you will enjoy every bit of it." He began again.

"*Nani's haveli* was huge, built in the form of a square. On the outer periphery were bedrooms in the north, two sets of kitchens, pantries, firewood stores and puja rooms, one of each on the east and the west sides. At the south end were two halls meant for men separated by a big entrance lobby from where the stairs rose to the terrace.

"In the centre of the *haveli* was a large courtyard, at least 50 feet by 50 feet. It had a cement floor and was used for cleaning, sorting and storing the crops of the season. *Nana* usually held his gossip sessions in an annexe which touched the northern wall of the *haveli*. He came inside the *haveli* only at dinner time. His breakfast and lunch were served in the annexe. Thus all of us, more than two dozen cousins and village boys, indulged in free-for-all riotous games in the centre courtyard. At times we played football or even rode on cycles. As the shadows of the setting sun lengthened and columns of smoke went up the hearths, all of us were cleaned up and rushed through the evening meal. This was the signal of *Nana's* dinner time.

"Prior to *Nana's* meal, the courtyard was swept or washed. My uncles and aunts finished their chores and gathered their broods to their respective bedrooms. Our beds were in *Nani's* bedroom, where our mother quietly laid us to sleep. No one cried or laughed. *Nana's* arrival into that empty, soundless but clean and open space, just after dark, was awaited with bated breath."

Ram Vilas paused for a while to check if Sonu was still awake. Finding him fully attentive, he continued, "I cannot forget that fateful day when, at the gossip session in the annexe, Shera, a well-known wrestler from the adjoining village, and *Nana* got into a heated argument. They decided to settle the issue with a wrestling bout. *Nana* and Shera immediately went towards the *akhara* (a wrestling square) in the centre of the village. They oiled their bodies and smeared themselves with the earth of the *akhara.*

"Soon they were grappling with each other. For well over half an hour they wrestled; at times, Shera got on top of *Nana*, at other times vice versa. Suddenly, *Nana* picked up Shera, hoisted him above his head and threw him flat on his back on the ground. There was a triumphant yell from the onlookers and *Nana* twirled his moustache in triumph."

Sonu also perked up and said, "Hurrah! *Dada*, you must have also shouted like this."

"Oh, yes, Sonu, I was dancing and jumping. I was mighty proud of my strong *Nana.*

"That very evening *Nana* came for his evening meal, which he enjoyed in the more or less quiet company of *Nani*. Perhaps they talked in that once a day get-together, but nothing was ever audible. *Nana* would go back to the annexe after the meal and *Nani* would come over to tell us a new story everyday.

"Sonu, listen carefully now," said Ram Vilas. "It was a bright evening. The silent courtyard was like a frozen platform of ice. *Nana* came in majestically as usual. I liked seeing his tall figure walk in. I saw him kick something and there was a shockingly loud thud on our door. I was terrified. He roared, 'There are so many of you here and still this place isn't maintained.'

"*Nana* ate his meal and *Nani* stayed quiet. My mother covered us with a quilt. Was there a storm coming? No. The bright evening became dark. *Nani* came in, and quite unflapped, narrated a new story. She must have told my mother of the entire episode but only after we had slept.

"The next day was no different except we were speedily tucked in our beds in the evening. The courtyard was washed and mopped dry. *Nani* called two servants and bade them to empty two bags of potatoes in the courtyard, spreading them from corner to corner. My little head failed to grasp this mystery.

Therefore, I waited for *Nana* to come in for dinner.

"Once again the night was moonlit but the courtyard was littered with potatoes. *Nana* froze in the doorway. He did not put a foot forward. After a while he called out, 'Vidya, come here, dear. Your mother, it seems, is angry with me because of last evening. I should not have kicked the potato. After all it is a home. I should have been considerate towards her.'

"My mother took her father carefully inside the kitchen where *Nani* spread out the dinner as usual. My mother could manage the truce. *Nana* was smiling when he left for the annexe. *Nani* too was cheerful.

"Sonu, I can never forget my *Nani's* wise ways. She won every battle, within the *haveli* or outside it, but always silently!"

The Land of the Lost
Arati Luthra Pinto

Raju loves to dig. He digs the soil in the morning, in the evening and, sometimes, at night as well. Afternoons are no-dig time, as his mother thinks the sun is too strong for her son. He digs with old pencils, his sand-spade, broken twigs or anything long and sharp he can find.

Raju loves the feel of soil especially when it is wet and squishy. In the soil he has often found worms, ants, old leaves, pieces of glass, stone, so many things. He believes there is a whole world living there. He often wonders what the underground world must be doing while he sits doing his homework.

Soil contains the magic that changes seeds into plants. Raju has often sown seeds like coriander and fenugreek and seen them burst out with roots and shoots and leaves. For Raju the underground world is an exciting and mysterious place, different from his world. So he digs and digs.

One day, as Raju was digging, he found he could dig no farther nor could he get his pencil out. He started digging the soil with his fingers. Suddenly, he saw some hair. Raju pulled at the hair and he heard a cry, "Don't do that. It hurts!"

Excitedly, Raju began loosening the soil. To his surprise, in the hole he had made stood a small boy—no bigger than his hand. To his greater surprise, the small boy looked just like him—the same curly hair, eyes and sparkling teeth.

"Who are you? Why do you look like me? What are you doing here, under the soil?" Raju asked 'Little Raju'.

"I will tell you my story," Little Raju replied. "Remember you lost your cycle key in the garden?"

"Yes, yes, I remember. I searched hard for it but I could not find it! Tell me, do you have my key?"

"No," said Little Raju. "I don't have your key, I am your key!"

"You? My key! You are fooling me. You are a boy, with hair and eyes and ears. My key was a silver one."

"Oh! I forgot. You don't know about the Land of the Lost!" replied Little Raju.

"The Land of the Lost? What are you talking about?" asked Raju, getting more and more interested in Little Raju's tale.

"The Land of the Lost is a place where all lost things live. They live not as the lost thing but as the person who lost them. So, in the Land of the Lost, your key has become you, that is me. My name is Raju Chaabi. Your mother's ear-ring is also there. She is a pretty girl, Priya Bali, and your friend, Balram's toy engine is also with us. He is called Balram Gaadi."

Fascinated by what he was hearing, Raju did not notice that Raju Chaabi was scrambling out of the hole and dusting himself.

"Where are you going?" asked Raju.

"Going? I am not going anywhere! I am coming with you," said Raju Chaabi.

"Coming with me, are you?" Raju was excited. "Won't your friends miss you?"

"We have a rule," said Raju Chaabi. "If we are found by our owners, we can spend a day with them. I have to return only at sunset today. What fun we can have together! You know, I

miss you. In your pocket I used to go to so many places. What I liked best was when you wore the key chain round your finger and I would dangle in the open air!"

Raju was bending down to listen to Chaabi's chatter. Chaabi quickly climbed up Raju's clothes and settled on his shoulder. Then he said, "Let me see your cycle. I would like to go for a ride on it!"

Raju took Chaabi for a ride around the garden on his cycle.

Then Raju got an idea. He asked Chaabi, "You climb well. Could you climb into my brother's cupboard and get me a bubble gum which he has hidden on the top shelf?"

Chaabi agreed, and was soon in the cupboard, climbing up. When he found the bubble gum, he tossed it to Raju. They shared it between themselves.

Then Raju got another idea. He called his friends to his house, telling them that he had learnt a new magic trick. The children sat on a mat in front of a curtain and Raju began his act.

He announced that he would become small when he ate unhealthy food, and would grow big when he ate healthy food. From behind the curtain he said, "I am now eating a banana," and tossed the peel at the children. He came in front as himself and showed his "big" size. Hiding behind the curtain, he said, "I am eating a chocolate bar," and sent a chocolate wrapper flying at the children. This time he sent Chaabi to the front.

The children were stunned. Some giggled in glee, others sat looking worried at what had happened to their friend. Raju repeated his act with various items of food. After every healthy food, he would present himself; after unhealthy food, he would send Chaabi.

The children could not believe what they had seen. When finally they left, thinking that Raju was a real magician, they promised to eat only healthy food.

Raju and Chaabi suddenly realized that soon the sun would set. They walked to the garden and found Chaabi's hole.

Chaabi hugged Raju's toe as he left saying, "You are a good friend, Raju. Take care of your things. The Land of the Lost is getting very crowded."

Now Raju is very careful not to overcrowd the Land of the Lost.

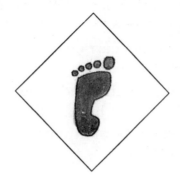

One Step at a Time
Cheryl Rao

"Papa, I am not going there again!" said Nilesh.

Mr. Patel did not reply. Nilesh felt uncomfortable.

"Rohan is a spoilt brat!" he muttered. "He keeps all the best G.I. Joe toys for himself and I have to be the enemy with only a few fighters and hardly any weapons! And half-way through the game, he makes new rules to suit himself!"

Mr. Patel remained silent.

"You are not listening, Papa," cried Nilesh.

"I have heard everything you have said," replied Mr. Patel.

"Then it is okay if I don't go there again, isn't it?"

"It is up to you, son," said his father. "I don't want to force you to do something you seem to detest so much."

Mr. Patel walked to the verandah and Nilesh followed. They stood and watched the stars. Mr. Patel spoke. "Whenever I look at the sky at night, I am reminded of how small and insignificant we are. Tiny blots of humanity, and yet how important we think we are. Must we live and die without making a difference to anyone or anything?"

Nilesh was puzzled. What did Papa mean? Why did he talk

in riddles? 'Anyway, I won't think of it. I was worried that Papa would force me to go to Rohan's house because he and Uncle Satpute are friends. Now I don't have to go. I will have more time for my batting practice.'

The next evening, Nilesh carried on playing in the park after six o'clock—the time he usually went to Rohan's house. He was batting well until he chanced to look in the direction of Rohan's house and thought he caught a glimpse of Rohan at the window. That brief lack of attention was his undoing. Off went the bails.

"Out!" shouted his friends.

Nilesh gave up the bat in disgust. An unfair thought flashed through his mind. 'It is all Rohan's fault. If I hadn't looked at him, I would still be batting.' He sat down on a stone to watch the rest of the match, but he could not concentrate. His eyes were drawn to Rohan's window. There was no one there.

Nilesh stood up and walked away quickly, after a word to his team-mates. When he reached Rohan's house and heard Mrs. Satpute say, "Rohan is waiting for you," a pang of guilt went through him.

Rohan had his back to the door. Slowly, he turned in his wheelchair and faced Nilesh. "Why did you leave the game? Did you get bowled out?" he asked gruffly.

Nilesh nodded. He thought he saw a trace of redness in Rohan's eyes. He could not be sure, for Rohan was looking at a toy in his hand. Had Rohan been crying because he, Nilesh, had not come at six, as usual?

The boys did not speak. Each waited for the other to say something first.

Mrs. Satpute entered. "Why, Rohan, you haven't asked Nilesh to sit down and play with you!"

Rohan shrugged. "It won't hurt him to stand for a while. He can help himself to the toys. That is why he is here, isn't he?"

Mrs. Satpute looked at Nilesh pleadingly, as if asking him

not to take offence. "Rohan is upset that you were late today," she explained.

"I am not upset!" cried Rohan, tossing the toy from his hand to the table. "I am quite happy on my own. I don't need favours!"

Nilesh noticed that Rohan's hand was trembling. He no longer felt annoyed by Rohan's rudeness, and the resentment that had been building up in him, evaporated. A wave of sympathy swept through him. 'Rohan must hate being confined to that wheelchair after his accident. No wonder he gets angry when he is kept waiting!'

With a smile, Nilesh said, "I will try not to be late again. I didn't think you would miss me."

"I didn't," muttered Rohan.

Nilesh knew that he was lying.

They sat down to a game of Boggle. Nilesh was beaten hollow. Though he knew plenty of words, for he was an avid reader, he was not in the same league as Rohan. "It is not fair!" said Nilesh in disgust. "You are a walking dictionary. I won't play any more word games with you!"

"Why?" challenged Rohan. "Can't you handle losing?"

Nilesh did not reply, but the words rankled. 'Rohan is right,' he thought as he jogged home. 'I am not a good loser. That is why Papa tells me to play all kinds of games, not just those that I am good at. He wants me to learn to lose gracefully.'

"Where were you?" asked Mr. Patel casually, when Nilesh reached home. "I didn't see you playing in the park when I passed by."

"I went to Rohan's house. You know I go there everyday."

"I thought you weren't planning to visit him again because he is a spoilt brat," commented his father.

"Oh, he is not so bad," admitted Nilesh shamefacedly. "We are getting on better now."

"Perhaps you are learning not to be too bossy and wilful yourself," said Mr. Patel mildly.

"Papa! I am not wilful!"

"No? I rather imagined that you liked having your own way and tried your best to get it. In fact, most people do. It is only as we go through life that we learn to be accommodating."

Nilesh reddened. Papa was right as usual.

The weeks flew by. Visiting Rohan became a habit. It was something Nilesh missed when he did not do it. Rohan did not get angry or upset when Nilesh failed to turn up on time. He too had learnt to have confidence in Nilesh's affection. Nilesh would turn up eventually to spend a few moments with Rohan and share the experiences of his day with the boy who was confined to the house.

Then came an upheaval in their lives. Rohan had to undergo an operation. If he was lucky, he would walk again. He had spent months in hospital after the accident. He did not want to enter one again, and dreaded the forthcoming operation.

"Maybe we will play cricket together soon," said Nilesh brightly, trying to cheer up his friend.

"Don't be silly. I may walk. I will never run again."

"If you can walk, you can bat. I will be your runner," insisted Nilesh. "I shall visit you in hospital as often as I can. I promise."

There was a lump in Nilesh's throat as he waved goodbye to his friend.

The half-yearly examinations began the following week and he was busy studying. He visited Rohan twice with his father for the hospital was far away. Each time Rohan was half-asleep, looking tired and pale. They had little to say to each other. Nilesh did not want to see Rohan looking the way he did— weak and lifeless, with all the animation gone from his eyes. He hated to think of Rohan struggling and suffering to take a step, when he, Nilesh, could walk, run and jump effortlessly.

The winter break came and Nilesh missed Rohan's company and Rohan's help with his projects. How easily Rohan had supplied him with information from his computer! 'I have learnt much from Rohan,' Nilesh realized. 'I have learnt to give and to take and, most of all, I have learnt to appreciate all I have.'

During the holidays, Nilesh accompanied Mrs. Satpute a couple of times to the hospital. Rohan was always busy with physiotherapists and Nilesh felt uncomfortable hanging around the corridors and watching hospital life.

Three months passed. Rohan had not returned. Nilesh missed him sorely. 'I thought that I was doing him a favour by visiting him. I didn't realize that I would find such a dear friend in him. Now that the companionship is gone, I know what I had. I wish I could get it back.'

Slowly, Nilesh allowed the memory of the old routine to fade and got used to being without Rohan. He completed Class VII. He was almost a senior. He was in charge of a group of younger boys for P.T. He had to move on. His trips to the hospital were infrequent. When Nilesh and Rohan met, they were awkward with each other. Rohan could not hope to make Nilesh understand the ordeal he was undergoing, and Nilesh felt foolish describing everyday happenings to him, when the prospect of walking—which most people took for granted—was what obsessed Rohan. It seemed that their close friendship had faded. Maybe they had outgrown each other.

One Saturday afternoon Nilesh stood outside Rohan's house. Mrs. Satpute had asked him to accompany her to the hospital. He walked to the door and rang the bell. Mrs. Satpute opened the door. She drew him in and they headed for the study.

Suddenly someone appeared in the doorway. A boy taller than Nilesh, with long hair curling over his collar, stood there. He did not smile. Slowly, he walked towards Nilesh, dragging one foot slightly as he moved. Nilesh was dumbstruck. Then he gave a whoop of joy. "Rohan! I didn't recognize you! You are so tall! So different!"

"Homo erectus at last," joked Rohan. "You haven't seen me upright like this, have you?"

Nilesh could not help himself. He took the last two paces between them in one jump and hugged Rohan tight, clapping him on the back and blinking rapidly all the while.

The old feeling came back. Their friendship was not lost. It stretched behind them and before them. They just needed to help each other find it, taking one step at a time.

The Runaway Engine
Girija Rani Asthana

It was a dark and rainy night.

It had been raining continuously for three days, sometimes a drizzle, at others a downpour. The platform of the railway station was deserted except for the porter and a linesman, both huddled around a fire trying to warm themselves against the bitter December cold. It was a small station. Not many trains stopped there, but, being on the main line, it was also an important station and prominent trains passed through it.

The Assistant Station Master, Mr. Shekhawat, was in his cabin, carefully making entries into a big ledger. Siddhartha was reclining in a big armchair and reading a book.

"Getting bored?" asked Mr. Shekhawat.

"Not at all. This book is really interesting, *Chachu* (father's younger brother). You have such a great collection of books, especially ghost stories!" Siddhartha exclaimed, wrapping the blanket tightly around him.

"Do you like ghost stories?" Mr. Shekhawat looked at him with amusement.

"I love them! The mystery and the adventure, the tinge of the

76

supernatural—something which cannot be explained logically."

"Aren't you afraid of ghosts? I have heard that this is the perfect kind of night for ghosts to venture out," Mr. Shekhawat tried to tease Siddhartha.

"*Chachu,* do you think I am a small child, that I will get scared of ghosts?" he protested at once. After a moment, he asked softly, "Are there really ghosts?"

"So I have heard from the local people. It seems that many years ago, a train plunged into the nearby river. A very unfortunate accident. Anyway, people say ghosts from that train sometimes visit the accident site," Mr. Shekhawat spoke in a serious tone. When he looked at Siddhartha's face he laughed loudly, "Ha ha ha...! No, Siddhartha, there are no ghosts in this 21st century! Okay, I am almost finished. As soon as I have entered these figures into this ledger, we will go to my quarters and eat. *Aloo paratha, kheer* and *matar paneer*—your aunt cooked up a storm before she left!"

"Take your time, I am not in a hurry," answered Siddhartha.

Ramnagar was a tiny station in the catchment area of Shivalik hills. It was on the main line from Delhi to Punjab. Ramnagar had two rivers—Markanda and Tangri. They were small rivers that usually got flooded during the rainy season. Siddhartha had come to spend his winter vacations here with his uncle. His parents had gone abroad for an academic conference. His aunt had had to go to her brother's place suddenly and Mr. Shekhawat did not want his nephew to remain alone in the house at night. So it was that Siddhartha was sitting in his uncle's cabin, reading ghost stories. He was feeling cramped sitting at one place and was dying to stretch his limbs. Just then he heard the faint sound of a train whistle.

"*Chachu,* I think I heard an engine whistle," said Siddhartha.

"Engine whistle? No way. There is no train for two and a half hours. The last train was the Saharanpur Passenger that passed through in the evening. The next train expected is the mail train going to Pathankot, and that will pass through only at midnight. Still a lot of time to go for it," Mr. Shekhawat replied looking at the chart spread on his table. As he finished his sentence, the shrill sound of an engine whistle filled the station. Mr. Shekhawat jumped up from his chair and ran out with Siddhartha at his heels.

The porter, Ganga Ram, and the linesman, Mehardin, stood there, open-mouthed, looking at each other in bewilderment. "An engine whistle! But...but...nnn...no...train is expected."

They all stared hard into the pitch dark night. In the pouring rain and inky darkness of the winter night they could not make out anything. Just then the sound of the whistle came again and then dhar...dhar...dhar...an engine entered the station, and before they could breathe, it was out of sight. All four of them looked at the engine disappearing into the dark night that it had suddenly appeared from. It took them some moments to absorb what they had seen.

"Where did that come from?" exclaimed Mr. Shekhawat.

"Sir, did you see that it was a steam engine, those that are out of use these days?" said Mehardin.

"*Chachu,* I did not see any driver. I am pretty sure that there was no driver in the engine," Siddhartha spoke agitatedly.

They all stood as if in a stupor. Then Mr. Shekhawat rushed into his office and rang up the nearest station. No, they did not know of any engine making unscheduled rounds of the area.

"I must inform the next junction about that runaway engine. In two hours the mail train will be here, and I don't want the two to collide." He got busy with his railway telephone.

"Mehardin, I am sure it is that ghost engine people talk about," Ganga Ram, the porter, spoke slowly. He was trembling with fear.

"What ghost engine, Ganga Ram *Kaka* (uncle)? Please tell me," pleaded Siddhartha.

"Don't scare the child, Ganga Ram!" admonished Mehardin.

"No, please, *Kaka*, tell me!" Siddhartha insisted.

"You see, many years ago, a train accident took place not far from here. The small bridge on the river Markanda was washed away by heavy rains. Nobody knew that. As soon as the engine of a passenger train climbed onto the bridge, it plunged into the swirling waters of the river below. Luckily the bogies got unhooked from the engine owing to the impact. Only the engine was affected. The driver and his assistant were never heard of again. All the passengers were miraculously saved. They say that, since then, whenever there is any danger on the railway track, the engine appears to warn against it."

"Has it ever averted any accident?" asked Siddhartha.

"God knows. People only talk, none know it for certain. Nobody has actually seen it before, I think. I don't know anyone who has seen it," said Ganga Ram.

Mr. Shekhawat came back. "We will have to go on the track and trace the engine. We cannot let the engine loose on this busy track. I have warned the other stations in the vicinity to stop all trains. Mehardin, bring the trolley."

In a moment Mehardin brought the inspection trolley. Ganga Ram brought two raincoats and a battery-operated searchlight. Mr. Shekhawat climbed onto the trolley.

"*Chachu*, may I also come? Please, *Chachu*, take me with you," Siddhartha pleaded.

Mr. Shekhawat thought for a moment. "All right, come on. What will you do here alone, anyway?" He instructed Ganga Ram to attend to the telephone.

Mehardin pushed the trolley and, when it picked up speed, climbed onto it. They switched on the big searchlight. The railway track and the surrounding area was bathed in the strong glare of its light. Luckily the rain had stopped. The wind was still strong and lashed at them. They travelled like this for some time. There was no sign of the runaway engine.

"How far are we from the station, Mehardin? We have been

travelling for at least fifteen minutes," asked Mr. Shekhawat, trying to hold the flapping ends of his raincoat tightly together.

"We are nearing the old bridge on Markanda river, Sir," answered Mehardin and rubbed his hands to warm them.

Siddhartha kept quiet. He was excited. Oh! What an adventure! There would be so much to tell in the class when school reopened, he thought.

Suddenly they heard the sound of gushing water and saw the runaway engine standing still on the railway track.

Mehardin applied the brakes. The trolley stopped. They quickly jumped down and walked gingerly towards the engine as if afraid that it would suddenly shoot off again. The sound of gushing water had changed into a roar now. The engine stood there as if it had been standing there like that for ages. When they reached the engine, they gasped. There were no rail tracks ahead! The bridge had been washed away and the swollen river was roaring below. Some remnants of the washed away bridge were still standing.

"Oh, my God!" exclaimed Mr. Shekhawat. "I shudder to think of what would have happened if, instead of this engine, it was the mail train!" Mr. Shekhawat looked at the engine. It was an old steam engine. Mehardin and Mr. Shekhawat looked at each other. Their faces were white as if they had seen a ghost.

"It is the same engine which was involved in the train accident many years ago. It has been standing unused for ages in the old railway scrapyard," Mr. Shekhawat spoke slowly.

"So people were right," whispered Siddhartha. "The runaway engine has indeed averted yet another mishap."

Roli and the Coin
Aradhna Jha

"Flowers for your miss! Take some flowers for your miss!" said the flower seller as he sat on the pavement with a large, brown, wicker basket.

Every morning he could be seen outside the school building, selling flowers to the children for five rupees a bunch.

The flower seller had left his family behind in the village and come to the city to earn a living. He could visit them only once or twice a year. He particularly missed his four-year-old daughter, Gudia. How he wished he could see her more often!

Little Roli was also four years old. She was a pretty girl with a dimple in her chin and a head full of curly hair. She often bought flowers before going to school. The flower seller liked her because she was always polite and well-behaved. But more so because she reminded him of his Gudia.

Roli liked her teacher and loved giving her flowers.

"Thank you, Roli," her teacher would say with a smile. "The flowers are lovely. Now let us arrange them in a vase."

Roli enjoyed this. The vase would then be placed on top of the class cupboard. How pretty the flowers looked up there!

82

As time went by, Roli began to ask her mother for flowers everyday, "Oh! Mama, please buy a bunch for me. My teacher will be very happy..."

Roli's mother was afraid that it would become a habit with her. "No, Roli, not today. You don't have to give flowers to your teacher everyday," she would say firmly.

Roli would insist. She just would not take a 'No' for an answer.

"Please, Mama," she would plead in her sweetest voice, "please let me buy some. My classroom looks nice with the flowers!"

Unable to argue further, her mother would give in. What else could she do with such a persuasive daughter?

One morning, however, Roli's mother had an idea. 'I won't take my purse to school today,' she thought. 'Then I will have no money to buy the flowers.'

As usual Roli stopped near the flower basket. Pointing to a small bunch of roses, she said, "Mama, may I have those?"

"Sorry, dear," replied her mother. "I haven't brought my purse today. I have no money to buy the roses."

Roli's face fell when she heard this. "Oh!" she said, very disappointed. There was nothing she could do. She quietly walked through the school gate, holding her mother's hand.

From that day, her mother stopped taking her purse to school. "Sorry, Roli," she would say. "No purse, so no flowers today."

Poor Roli! How she missed buying the colourful little bouquets! Every morning she would stop near the basket and stare longingly at them. Then she would look hopefully at her mother who would always give the same excuse.

"Flowers for your miss! Won't you buy some flowers for your miss?" the flower seller would tempt her.

Roli would just shake her head and walk away silently.

One evening Roli was busy at home playing with her little red car. It was her favourite toy, given to her by her father some months earlier.

"Zoom, zoom, zoom!!" she cried giving it a hard push. The

little battery-operated red car sped away along the smooth, white floor.

Roli ran after it until it stopped. As she bent down to pick it up, she saw something round and shiny lying next to the car.

It was a one rupee coin.

"Oooh, a new coin!" squealed Roli with delight. She grabbed it at once and examined it closely. Suddenly a wonderful thought struck her.

"Mama!" she cried in a shrill voice.

"What is it, dear?" said her mother looking up from the book she was reading.

Roli burst into the room, her soft, brown curls bobbing up and down.

"Mama, look what I found," she said, her eyes shining like stars. Slowly she stretched out her right hand. On the little palm lay a bright new coin.

"Oh!" said her mother. "Where did you find it?"

"It was lying on the floor in my room," replied Roli looking very pleased. "Mama, may I keep it?"

"Yes, of course, but what will you do with it?" asked her mother curiously.

"I will buy flowers for my teacher tomorrow," said Roli.

"A bunch of flowers with a one rupee coin?" her mother asked.

"Yes, a bunch of pretty pink roses," declared Roli. Then she skipped out of the room, her curls merrily bouncing away on her head.

Roli's mother was thoughtful for a while, 'Should I explain to Roli that she won't get flowers for one rupee? On second thoughts,' she smiled, 'let her try to buy a whole bunch of roses with that coin tomorrow! Roli is growing up, she must learn the value of money.'

That night Roli carefully put away the coin in a drawer. She took it out the next morning and popped it into the pocket of her white school uniform.

84

"Let us go, Mama," she said enthusiastically.

Roli stopped outside the school gate and eyed the flower-laden basket. Her mother said nothing. She stood by watching.

Roli selected a small bunch of dark pink roses.

"I want those roses," she told the flower seller, pointing a plump little finger towards them.

"Yes, of course, *beti*," he said, smiling. "You are taking flowers for your miss today after a long time."

Roli nodded and took the roses eagerly. Then she buried her face into the soft, pink petals and took a long, deep breath.

Aaah! What a lovely, sweet scent they had! And how beautiful they looked!

"I am afraid Roli, you can't have them..." Her mother began to say.

The little girl looked up at her mother with a twinkle in her eyes. Then she said with great confidence, "You don't have to pay, Mama. Today I will buy the flowers with my own money—with my own coin."

"All right, Roli," said her mother smiling. She felt quite sorry for Roli as she knew what was going to happen. The man would return her one rupee coin and take back his flowers.

'Poor Roli will be so disappointed!' thought her mother to herself. 'After all she is only four years old and doesn't really know how much a rupee is worth. But she will learn an important lesson today. She will learn the real value of money.'

While her mother was lost in her thoughts, Roli had carefully taken out the coin from her pocket. With a shy smile, she dropped it into the outstretched palm of the flower seller.

The man stared at the one rupee coin. He was taken aback. He looked up at the smiling face of the girl.

Roli was looking at him expectantly. She was determined to take flowers for her teacher that morning. And she would buy them with her own money! Thinking about this, her face glowed with happiness and pride.

The flower seller stared at the coin once more. He looked at the small figure standing quietly opposite him, looking so happy and hopeful.

Suddenly the thought of Gudia crossed his mind. He had been really missing her the last few days. How he longed to see her again and play with her! How he missed her innocent chatter and tinkling laughter!

At that moment, he saw not Roli but his own daughter standing there, stretching out her little hand to take the flowers.

The flower seller was overwhelmed. He said nothing, just nodded his head and dropped the coin into his shirt pocket.

Overcome, he said, "*Beti*, take these roses. They are the best I have." He turned his attention to another customer.

"Mama, look!" cried Roli happily. "I got the flowers with my coin!" Looking radiant, she held up the roses.

Her mother was truly amazed. How had Roli managed to get a bunch of beautiful roses for only a rupee? She had no answer to the question. One thing was certain. Little Roli had turned the tables on her!

Giving her a quick hug she said, "The roses are lovely, dear. Let us go." She led her towards the school.

The flower seller stared after Roli as she walked away, his eyes brimming with tears. It was he who knew the real value of the coin. To him it was worth much more than a rupee. In fact, it was priceless.

For, was it not given to him by his own little Gudia?

Ajji's *Temporary Amnesia*

Madhavi Mahadevan

Neel was on his way to school. It was a beautiful morning—clear, blue skies, a cool breeze. Neel enjoyed this daily walk. At this early hour, Ganesh Temple Street was quiet and uncrowded. Later, it would be a totally different place.

Neel's grandmother, his *Ajji*, had told him that there was a time when every house in their street had a big garden. Birdsong and the ringing of temple bells were the only noise they heard. Then the big builders moved in. "Such a centrally located area," they said. "Prime property."

One by one, the old houses were pulled down and replaced by luxury condominiums, posh shopping malls and swank offices. Trees were cut; the birds fled. With a big bang, the world discovered Ganesh Temple Street.

One tiny corner of it remained unchanged. *Ajji* refused to sell to the builders. They raised their offers. *Ajji* raised her voice, explicitly telling the builders what they could do with their money. They retreated, secure in the knowledge that they had merely lost a battle, not the war.

Ajji's victory was a hollow one. Her family—her two sons,

their wives and children—had loved hearing what the builders had to offer. Suddenly they began dreaming of fast cars and holidays abroad. *Ajji* had sent all those dreams crashing.

"Typical of *Ajji*," they muttered. "She is an enemy of progress. She is a dictator. Just look at the laws in this house. No loud music. No TV. No film magazines. No eating out. No staying out late. She is outdated. One must move with the times."

Ajji heard the mutterings. It made her see red.

Just that morning, there had been a terrible clash. In general, no one crossed swords with *Ajji*. She had a cutting tongue. A head-on confrontation usually led to the other party being cut down to size. Even so, Sapna, Neel's eighteen-year-old cousin, had decided to challenge *Ajji*.

One of the things that *Ajji* was proud of was hair. Sapna's hair. Long, glossy, straight—just the way *Ajji* liked it. She did not let anyone handle that hair, not even Sapna's mother, Ila. *Ajji* oiled Sapna's hair, combed it and plaited it herself. Ever since Sapna had started college, she had been campaigning to have her hair cut.

"No," *Ajji* said. "Never."

"It is my hair," Sapna stormed. "What I do with it is my business. You are infringing on my right."

"Rights are for those who know the difference between right and wrong," *Ajji* said. "It is not correct to argue with your elders."

Sapna stalked off.

The morning's clash had upset *Ajji* more than she let on.

She went about her chores, her mind elsewhere. 'I shouldn't have been so harsh with the child,' she thought. 'But if I am not firm, everyone will do as they like. The Raos of Ganesh Temple Street will be history.'

Ajji's fears were not unfounded. The builders had approached her sons with irresistible offers. *Ajji* did not know how long she could hold out. To think things out, she went into the garden, to her favourite spot under the coconut trees.

She looked around, seeing, as if for the first time, the wilderness about her. They could not get a gardener. When there were cushier jobs to be had, nobody wanted this one. The house too was in a bad shape. The roof leaked, the doors creaked, the walls rumbled, the plumbing grumbled.

"Sell, sell, sell," the voice in her head said.

No, *Ajji* argued. She had spent six decades in this house. In it she had known joy and sorrow, birth and death. So many she had loved and respected had lived here. All her vast past was linked with this house.

Ajji mulled over things for a long time. She reached a decision.

Ajji got up. By some inexplicable coincidence, a coconut detached itself from the cluster high above and came hurtling down. Fortunately, it was not a very big coconut. The round, plump bun at the back of *Ajji's* head cushioned the impact. However it knocked the wind out of *Ajji*. She gasped and sat down again. Then she got up and tottered indoors. She made it to the front door. Then she simply blanked out.

An hour later, she came to. She was flat on the floor. Three faces looked down at her, each mirroring concern.

"Who are you?" *Ajji* asked the oldest, a middle-aged lady in a pink sari. The lady's jaw dropped.

"*Amma*, I am your daughter-in-law, Ila," she replied timidly. "Don't you know me?"

Ajji frowned. "Daughter-in-law? Do I have one?"

She looked at the next face. It belonged to a ten-year-old boy. Anticipating the question, the boy said, "I am Neel, your grandson. I study in Class V. We, you and I, share a room."

"That is nice," *Ajji* said faintly. Her head was throbbing. She looked at the third and last person, a young girl with a look of scared defiance on her face.

"Do I know you?" *Ajji* asked in the same polite tone.

For some reason that harmless question upset the girl. Her face crumpled. *Ajji* looked bewildered.

"This is Sapna, your granddaughter," Neel introduced. "She is crying because she has gone and cut her hair." He added helpfully, "After you told her not to."

"Shut up," Sapna glared at Neel.

"Nice haircut," *Ajji* said quite unexpectedly. "Suits your face. I like it."

There was a stunned silence. Ila broke it.

"Oh, God!" she wailed. "I am calling the doctor." She got up, adding, "Don't leave her alone."

"Temporary amnesia," the doctor said. "Loss of memory. She has had a blow of some kind. There is a lump the size of a coconut at the back of her head."

"Will she be normal again?" *Ajji's* sons asked.

"Oh, yes. It may take a few days though. We will keep her under observation for forty-eight hours."

Ajji's sons were relieved. It was rather unnerving having to introduce yourself to your own mother. They too needed time to recover from the experience.

Two days later, *Ajji* was back home. She still remembered nothing of the past. Old friends came and introduced themselves; some old enemies, too. *Ajji* was nice to everyone.

One by one, all the laws she had laid down were broken. Pop music blared from dawn to dusk. *Ajji* seemed to love it as much as her grandchildren. After a few days, most elders were complaining of deafness and headache, not *Ajji*.

The TV was on till all hours. The children overslept and got into trouble for incomplete homework.

The whole family ate out. Chinese, one day, Mughlai, the next, pizzas on the third day. On the fourth, however, they stayed at home.

"Enough," Ila declared. "We are not used to fast living." She switched off the music system and the TV. Then, she went into the kitchen to make curd-rice for everyone.

*   *   *

One fine morning, the family found *Ajji* in the garden. She was sweeping the dead leaves. By now they had come to expect erratic behaviour from her. They asked very gently, "*Ajji*, what are you doing?"

"Cleaning up," she said, and pulled out a weed. "Why don't you join me?"

They looked at one another, shrugged their shoulders and got down to work. Then the roof was repaired, new plumbing installed. The house got a fresh coat of paint. It began to look quite nice. A photographer from the local daily came to take photographs of it. "Among the city's gracious old homes," the article said.

The builders too returned. This time, *Ajji's* sons sent them away. "We are not selling," they said.

In time, everyone got used to *Ajji's* amnesia, to the new *Ajji*.

'Why not cash in on it?' thought Basappa, the milkman. He had been supplying milk to the family for ten years. He was as scared of *Ajji* as anyone else. She had a razor-sharp memory. She kept the milk account in her head, down to the last paise.

On the first of the month, wily Basappa said, "*Ajji*, you owe me six hundred rupees." It was a good fifty rupees more than the actual figure.

Ajji's hand, which was at her purse, stopped. She looked at Basappa. Her eyes narrowed.

"What?" she asked as if she had suddenly lost her hearing as well.

"Six hundred rupees," the foolhardy man insisted.

Ajji's eyes turned into hot coals. They bore through the milkman. "Basappa!" she thundered.

The hapless man trembled.

"*Ajji*...you remember?" he whispered.

Ajji nodded.

"I am sorry," Basappa babbled. "A mistake...Five hundred and fifty."

Ajji handed him the amount.

Ajji smiled to herself. Nobody had seen what had happened. She was wrong. There was a witness. Neel.

Ajji was shocked to see him standing there, right behind her. For a long moment neither spoke. Neel was trying to understand what he had witnessed.

"*Ajji*!" he gasped. "You remember!"

"Yes," *Ajji* replied softly. "I remember."

"Everything?"

She nodded. A doubt crossed Neel's mind. He looked at her suspiciously. "Did you really lose your memory? You were not acting, were you?"

Though *Ajji* looked outraged at the suggestion, Neel saw the twinkle in her eyes.

"I lost my memory for a few hours," she admitted. "When I woke up in the hospital, everything came back to me. I decided to go on pretending for a while, specially when I saw the way all of you were reacting. It was a good opportunity to let bygones be bygones, I thought. To make a fresh start. I saw how eagerly old enemies came to patch up. It was a nice feeling. It is never too late to forgive and forget, is it?"

"And now?" Neel wanted to know. "Will you tell?"

"That depends on you," *Ajji* said. "What do you suggest?"

Neel thought for a moment. "Let us keep it a secret," he said. "Do you think that is a good idea?"

"Excellent," *Ajji* smiled. "So, it is our secret. Yours and mine."

And now, it is yours as well.

My Father's Wife
Deepa Agarwal

"This is Nita Aunty," Papa said as I opened the door.

Nita Aunty stood behind him, smiling nervously. I wondered why she was nervous. After all she was much older to me. She was tall, almost as tall as Papa. She was wearing a maroon cotton sari with an off-white border. Her short hair was tied back. She had a huge maroon *bindi* to match her sari.

Who was she? A relative I had never met before, or a friend of Mummy's who had never come to the house? Papa told me right away.

"She works with me in my office."

Office! Then what was she doing at home? That too on a Sunday. A sudden suspicion pinched my heart. Surely Papa could not be planning to work at home today, after promising to take me out for a picnic?

"Papa!" I cried out immediately in protest.

Papa frowned, then quickly turned it into a smile. An artificial one which made me even more suspicious. "Richa," he said, "aren't you going to ask Nita Aunty to sit down, offer her a glass of water?"

It was my turn to frown. I wanted to shout that it was not fair, that he was supposed to take me out, that he had broken his promise. I controlled myself somehow and turned towards the kitchen. I had the satisfaction of seeing Nita Aunty's smile wilt, her face pale and the apprehensive look she threw at Papa.

He followed me into the kitchen. "We are still going for the picnic, if that is what you are worried about," he said, his face serious. "Nita Aunty's coming too. I want you to behave nicely, or she will think Mummy never taught you anything..."

Tears started up in my eyes. It was almost a year since Mummy had gone...died... There, I have said the word. After all this time I guess I can face it. But at that time any mention of her made me want to cry. I felt it was particularly cruel of Papa to say such a thing. He realized it too. Probably he said it without thinking, because I saw the sudden pain jump into his eyes. He hugged me at once, saying hoarsely, "I am sorry, I didn't mean to hurt you...I can never do things right."

That made me feel worse. I had been thinking only of myself, not him. He must be having some good reason for asking Nita Aunty to join us for a picnic, I thought. It was foolish of me to jump to the conclusion that it was cancelled without asking him. I was not a little kid. I was twelve. Next year I would be a teenager. I snivelled a little into his shirt for a minute, then quickly controlled myself remembering Nita Aunty who must be wondering what was taking us so long. I quickly poured out something to drink, put on a bright smile and went out.

She was sitting stiffly on the sofa. I offered her the drink, then said in the pleasant way I had seen Mummy make conversation with people she was meeting for the first time, "I am glad you are coming with us for the picnic."

Her face brightened at once. "So am I," she said and opened the packet she was carrying. "I hear you are fond of reading," she continued. "I-I brought a few books for you."

Nancy Drews, Sweet Valleys, a couple of titles by Indian

authors. How had she managed to get all my favourite books? Of course, Papa must have told her. Why was she eager to please me? All these books. Just a couple would have been enough. Even a box of chocolates on top of it! That suspicious feeling somehow took the pleasure of the gift away.

"Ma," Papa yelled out to *Dadi*. "Nita is here."

Dadi also knew about her! What was going on?

No, I should not act like that. Papa may have forgotten to tell me. I had been sleeping when he left the house. How could he have told me?

I tried to enjoy the picnic. I did it for Mummy. So that Papa could not say that Nita Aunty would think that she had not taught me anything. It was hard, really hard, because no matter how much she smiled and tried to joke with me, I did not like Nita Aunty at all. I did not know whether it was because I had not known about her coming, or because I did not like the way she looked at Papa, as if they were really close friends, even more, the way *he* looked at her. I really wanted to scream and hit them both. Of course, I did not. How could I let Mummy down, after all?

It is not hard to pretend to be nice to someone you do not like, once in a while. If you have to do it all the time, it becomes harder and harder. Nita Aunty began to come very often to our house after that. She came for dinner, she went to the movies with us, she took me out shopping, for a haircut, she even came just like that, for no reason at at. *Dadi* became quite fond of her. Papa, of course, already was. But I, who was almost about to burst with being nice, could not stand her at all. Even though she tried hard to butter me up.

One day, I caught her looking at Mummy's photograph, the big one in the drawing room. "Your mother was very pretty," she said softly. "Just like you."

I knew she was a great big liar, then. Everyone said I looked like Papa.

Even then I managed to hold on, keeping all the bad feelings down. Till the day I came into drawing room and heard Papa and *Dadi* talking softly. I stood still for a moment. Perhaps they were talking about something they did not want me to hear. Well, if it was something like that, I definitely wanted to know it. I stood as quiet as a mouse and strained my ears for all I was worth and this is what I heard. "... Richa seems to like her..." My face burned when I heard that. I could guess whom they were talking about. I had acted too well! The next words turned me cold as ice. "She will make a good mother to her..."

For a moment I felt as though I had turned to stone. Then I crept back to my room. My heart was like a cold, hard lump inside me. My ears were buzzing. I wanted to be dead too like Mummy. Dead or far away. I hated Papa, I hated *Dadi* and, most of all, I hated Nita Aunty. My tears gushed out hot and hard. I could hear *Dadi* calling me. I pretended not to hear...

Dead or far away...Suddenly an idea sprang into my head. I could go to *Nani's* house. She would understand how I felt. I could not stay here where they were already planning to replace Mummy. For me, no one else could take her place and no one would. I could stay with *Nani*. They would probably be glad to have me out of the way. I am sure Nita Aunty would. Luckily I had plenty of cash. My Diwali money, birthday gifts. Usually Papa put it into the bank for me. But he had been very busy and had been forgetting. I quickly stuffed some clothes into a knapsack. I knew the time the train to *Nani's* place left. We had been on it often enough. Mummy and I.

I crept out silently through the back door. No one saw me go. I managed to buy a ticket and get onto the train. One or two persons did give me odd looks. Luckily I look big for my age.

"*Nani!*" I cried out as soon as she opened the door, and burst into tears.

She did not say anything, just listened quietly as I told her everything. To my surprise, she only sighed and made no comment when I told her about their wanting to replace Mummy. She said, "Of course, you can stay with me. You can stay with me as long as you wish."

Then she got busy fixing something for me to eat. I was feeling satisfied and drowsy and ready for bed when a sudden thought struck me. I should have left a letter for Papa to tell him what I was doing. He must be out of his mind worrying, wondering where I had gone. No, he must be happy to get rid of me now that he wanted to marry Nita Aunty... The thought kept nagging at me, till I asked *Nani*, "Do you think...you should call Papa?"

"I already have," she said, looking me straight in the eye. "I knew he would be really worried and upset."

"I am not sure about that," I said sulkily.

"Well, I am," she said firmly. "You are the most precious person in the world to him, specially after your mother passed away. And if this Nita Aunty is such a terrible person, your Papa is too smart a man to get fooled for long."

I sat up at once. "I never said that she was a terrible person..."

"You said you hated her; I assumed she must be really terrible because you are such a loving child."

Yes, I hated Nita Aunty, but was she such a terrible person? Actually...actually she was not that bad. And I had not always been nice to her. Only when Papa was around. I had given her a hard time when we went shopping, refusing to make up my mind about anything, condemning whatever she suggested. She had remained patient and smiling. It was the same way with the haircut. I had fussed and fussed but she had remained cool. If I had been in her place I would have given me a slap.

"No," I said slowly, "she is okay, she is...she is quite nice." They were the hardest words I had said, but Mummy had taught me to be fair. I was not going to let her down now.

"Then," said *Nani*, "have you thought about your Papa? He is quite young. You will grow up and go away. He will have to spend the rest of his life alone."

I flushed. I had not thought of that. I thought of Papa as a lonely old man and did not like it. However, I was not ready to give in easily.

"Nobody can take Mummy's place," I said stubbornly.

"Of course. She should not even try to. She should have a place of her own and you should allow her to."

"I allow her? Who is asking me?"

"You silly little girl, don't you realize your father will never do anything against your wishes?"

Yes, I was a silly little girl. I did not realize how silly till Papa arrived the next day. He hugged me till I thought my ribs would break. He cried, he actually cried, my father. I felt horrible. All shaky and trembly inside.

"Why did you do it?" he asked. "You know I have been out of my mind with worry. I could not bear the thought of losing you. Don't you know? No one is as important as you."

"Not even Nita Aunty?" I wanted to ask. I stopped myself. It was not the sort of thing Mummy would have said. What would she have said if she had been in this position? She never had; I had to figure it out of myself.

I said, "I am really sorry, Papa. I must be the dumbest girl in the world. I never meant to hurt you."

He hugged me again, his cheek rough and scratchy against mine. He had not even shaved.

"And, Papa," I went on, "I want to ask you something..."

"What?" he murmured. "Anything to make you happy..."

"I want you to marry Nita Aunty as fast as possible!"

The look on his face was enough. I knew that Mummy, wherever she was, would be proud of me. I had learned my lesson well.

Battle of the brains

Vandana Kumari Jena

Ravish was a quiet, young boy who studied in Class IX in a prestigious school in Delhi. Diminutive and lean, with horn-rimmed glasses, he exuded an air of studiousness which made him a respected member of his class. He had combined intelligence with diligence, and his hard work had certainly paid off because ever since he joined school he had consistently stood first. Anybody who joined his class and aimed to topple him was doomed to disappointment. Ravish took his studies so seriously that he never had much time for games, reading and other things. To him they were a waste of time. Most of his class-mates were very impressed with him, specially his best friend, Adesh, who always found it difficult to do the simplest of sums! Ravish was the teachers' favourite and his parents' pet. Life was quite simply heaven.

Into this paradise, however, soon came a serpent in the guise of a new boy, Varun. He was everything Ravish was not. Although just fourteen years old, he stood five feet eight inches in his socks. He was also athletic with bulging biceps. His prowess in sports was displayed on the first day itself when he

102

ran and won the 400-metre race with ease. He also turned out to be a brilliant footballer and a most powerful swimmer.

Ravish was impressed. Being poor at sports he could be generous with someone who excelled at it. After all Ravish's forte was studies and not sports.

Ravish did not feel particularly threatened when the school debate competition was announced and Varun decided to take part in it. Ravish had never participated in debates because he was painfully shy. He merely envied Varun who strode up on stage and lambasted the students who argued that "too much freedom spoils a child". Arguing that freedom enables a child to assume responsibility and become independent and is a boon rather than a curse, Varun won the big Nehru Memorial Trophy. Ravish knew that his turn would come when he would win a prize for standing first in the entire Class IX.

Imagine his shock when he discovered that Varun was brilliant in academics too! Although he was happy-go-lucky by nature and not serious about his tests, he soon started tying for the first place with Ravish. The first time Varun got higher marks than Ravish, he was convinced that Varun had cheated. He implied as much to his friend, Adesh, who gossiped about it to some friends. Nobody, however, believed it anymore when Varun solved a difficult sum which both the class teacher and Ravish had been unable to solve.

"My time will come," Ravish chanted to himself.

He thought it had when the annual essay competition was announced. The topic was announced beforehand but the children had to write the essay in class. Each class wrote on the topic and the best essay from each class was shortlisted for the prize. Ravish wrote excellent essays and had won several cups for them. When he turned in his essay he was sure he would win.

When the teacher came to class the next day she said, "I have to choose one entry from this class. Although I haven't read all the entries, in my opinion Varun's will, undoubtedly, be the best."

Ravish was stunned into silence. The class teacher had not even discussed the possibility of his essay being selected!

When he walked to the Staff Room to keep the classwork exercise books on the teacher's desk, he saw the essay competition entries. The green-eyed monster reared its ugly head. Before he even realized what he was doing, he had taken Varun's essay and torn it to bits. Then guilt assailed him and he was overcome with fear. What if anyone had seen him? What should he do with the torn bits of paper? He quickly went to the toilet and flushed them. He sagged with relief and was rather pale when he re-entered the classroom.

"What is the matter, Ravish? You seem unwell," Varun asked with concern.

"No," muttered Ravish, feeling ashamed of what he had done. A little demon danced within him and said, "With Varun out of the way, you are bound to win!"

The next day the teacher discovered the loss of the essay, and no amount of searching could help retrieve it. "In case the essay is not found, I will not send any entry from this class," threatened the teacher.

Varun found a solution to the problem. Although it had been an 'on-the-spot essay competition', he said he could rewrite the entire essay. Indeed, soon he had done it.

"How did you manage to do it?" marvelled the teacher.

"I guess I am lucky, Ma'am," Varun said modestly. "I have a photographic memory."

Ravish simply seethed with rage. When Varun walked away with the trophy which Ravish thought rightly belonged to him, he could no longer contain his jealousy. As the examinations approached, Ravish began to feel more panicky. It was just not fair. While it took him hours and hours to learn history and geography, Varun could learn it in a wink. That left him with

enough time for games and reading and computers. A week before the examinations when he spotted Varun's familiar red school bag, something snapped within him. He took out all his notes and hid them.

Varun discovered the loss of his bag and a hue and cry was raised. The bag was eventually found in the bathroom but the exercise books were missing. Varun seemed to be in tears.

"He is such a nice boy. Who could be so nasty to him?" the teacher wondered aloud.

Everyone displayed disbelief.

The next day onwards Varun stopped coming to school. 'Must be grieving over the loss of his books,' thought Ravish. 'Let us see how his photographic memory comes to his rescue.' When the next day too he did not come, Ravish started feeling nervous. By the third day he was positively tortured. He had visions of Varun wasting away in grief, unable to give the Class IX examinations and dying. He did not want Varun to die. In fact, he admitted to himself, Varun was a nice and jolly boy. It was only Ravish's jealousy that made him seem like a monster.

Ravish decided to go to Varun's house and take along his notes. But Varun lived far away. He could go only if his parents dropped him there. That meant telling his parents the truth. He was sure they would be furious. But it was necessary if he had to save Varun's life. He was prepared for any punishment from his or Varun's parents or from his school. He could not let an innocent child die.

When he told his parents about it, they heard him in silence and merely said, "Let us go and see Varun first."

When they went to Varun's house, he was nowhere to be seen. His parents were at home.

"My son has something to say to you," said Ravish's father.

Ravish blurted out the whole truth, of how he had felt that Varun had dethroned him and how he had sought his petty revenge. "Where is Varun?" he asked timidly, fearing that he would be in bed with raging fever or worse.

"He was afraid of something like this happening. He made me photocopy all his notes," laughed his father.

Just then Varun walked into the room looking pale and tired. Ravish tendered his apology to Varun, who did not seem surprised at all. Ravish realized that Varun must have realized all along that he was the culprit. He had the generosity not to betray him. Even at this moment he said, "It must have taken real courage to confess. I doubt if I could have done it."

'I doubt if you could stoop so low,' thought Ravish silently. 'You are a real sportsman.'

"You look very tired," said Ravish's mother sympathetically to Varun.

"He has been studying very hard," muttered his mother.

"But he has a photographic memory," blurted Ravish.

"Photographic! Not at all. Who told you?" Varun asked.

"Then how could you reproduce the essay?" countered Ravish.

"Simple. We had been told the topic beforehand. I was able to memorize it!" laughed Varun.

"How do you excel in many activities?" asked Ravish's mother.

"I believe there is a time for study and a time to play. I make sure Varun does both," said his mother.

"He has inherited his prowess in sports from me," boasted Varun's father. "I was a champion in sports."

Ravish sighed with relief. Varun did not have a superior gift. He was just an able competitor. Someone with whom it would be interesting to compete. Someone who would be worth emulating. Someone who would be a good friend.

He thought how surprised the class would be when they walked to the examination hall not as enemies but as friends. The prospect of standing second had lost its threat. Instead the thought of pitting his wits against a worthy opponent had become a challenge!

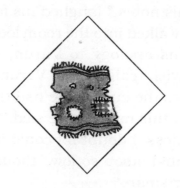

The Shawl
Lata Kaku

"Manjari! Hey, Manjari!" hailed the children, "where is your Ramprasad?" They laughed and chuckled, trailing a dishevelled Manjari as she walked towards the outskirts of the village.

Normally, no one teased Manjari, a harmless, deranged young girl. With kindness, born of pity, the village elders held her as a collective responsibility. Children often played with her. However, a cheeky new kid in flashy clothes was leading the children today.

Manjari turned a bewildered face to the group of children following her and intoned, "Ramprasad? My Ramprasad? Have you seen him? He must be feeling cold." She looked around frantically and her dirt-streaked face started to crumple as tears welled up in her eyes.

The children were silenced by this change. Her obvious distress made them feel ashamed. For a while, they stood shuffling their feet and then quietly slunk away.

Surajchand, who had watched all this from his grocery shop nearby, hurried up to Manjari.

By this time, tears were pouring down Manjari's face and

soaking her dress. "Ramprasad," she wailed.

Surajchand gently drew Manjari's tatty shawl around her shoulders, saying soothingly, "Maybe Ramprasad is just having a drink of water from the canal. Why don't you go and see? And also wash yourself there, all right?"

Feeling comforted, Manjari nodded and wandered off towards the canal. The air still had a nip in it although winter was almost at an end. Manjari pulled her shawl closer. She was so attached to the shawl that she rarely moved without it.

As always, the thrill of seeing the undulating, yellow mustard flowers in the fields and the canal itself made her forget her misery. She slid down the embankment and, sitting on the edge, splashed her feet in the water.

After a while, Manjari became aware of voices. She got up and followed the sounds. It led her almost to the point where the canal abutted the road, which was the village's link to the world beyond.

Peering from behind some bushes, Manjari saw a group of young boys and girls playing with a big ball. Their attire indicated that they were not of her village. The bicycles standing nearby told her how they had come. Baskets and boxes rested on a *durri* (cotton carpet) spread on the grass.

As Manjari continued to watch curiously, the boys and girls sat down around the baskets. One by one, they were opened and their contents taken out.

Food! Manjari's mouth watered. It was a long time since she had eaten and the sight of food made her feel hungry. She approached the group. The chattering stopped and everyone stared at her.

"What do you want?" one of the boys called out.

Manjari held out a hand. "I am hungry," she said simply.

The boy looked at her unkempt hair, dirty clothes and bare feet. He did not like what he saw. "Go away from here," he waved at her.

109

Manjari came nearer still. "Give me something to eat," she repeated petulantly.

The girls felt scared. One of them quickly picked up a couple of sandwiches and thrust them at her.

Manjari grabbed them and started eating. "More," she demanded loudly.

This annoyed the boys and they threatened her. Frightened, she backed off. She went back to the bushes and watched covertly from there as long as the food lasted. Once that was over, she lost interest and turned away.

Now the water again beckoned her. She took off her tattered shawl, placed it carefully high up on the embankment, and waded into the water which came almost upto her knees. The sun was very bright and Manjari enjoyed the coolness of the water as she splashed around.

"Ramprasad, it is very nice here," she said. "You like it, don't you? It will be cold afterwards. Don't worry at all. I have my shawl. We shall wrap it around ourselves and neither of us will feel cold." Many times she cupped water in her hands and threw it at something and chortled.

A little distance away, the boys and girls continued playing.

The shadows had started lengthening when Ranjeet called out, "I say, guys, isn't it time we started back?"

A groan went up. The players consulted their watches and agreed that it was time to pack up and start back.

The boys collected the various items and passed them to the girls, who stacked them neatly into the baskets. These were carried to the backs of bicycles, where the boys started lashing them onto the carriers.

Suddenly, Amit said, "Has anyone seen the rope for this basket? I can't seem to find it."

"No...oo," answered a few voices.

"Monty, Billu, Dolly, help me look for the rope. Else, how shall I tie this to my bike?" Amit called out to his friends.

"Let us look around. Maybe we will find something else to tie the basket with," suggested someone.

So, in twos and threes, they started hunting.

"What about this?" asked someone, mockingly holding up a long straw.

"Ha... ha, very funny," retorted Amit.

"Hurry up, find something," pleaded Dolly. "I must get back before dark."

Ranjeet, moving farther away from the others, came to the canal where Manjari was still splashing. The threadbare, yellow shawl on the bank caught his attention.

"This will do nicely," he muttered to himself.

He glanced at Manjari and shrugged. Ranjeet came from a well-to-do family. His wardrobe and shoes were admired by his friends. He replaced shirts at the drop of a button. This yellow piece of rag could not be of any serious use, he thought. He waved to Manjari.

"Hey there, I am taking this rag and here is Rs. 10 for it," he said, taking the shawl and placing the note in its place.

"No," shouted Manjari, as she slowly realized that her shawl was being taken away.

"All right, here is Rs. 50. You can get a better one," responded Ranjeet, seeing the agitated look on Manjari's face. He could not imagine how anyone could value such a rag which was already falling to pieces. He placed the money under a rock and hurried back without looking at Manjari again, tearing the shawl into strips as he went.

Manjari waded out of the water and stood on the bank, staring at the rapidly retreating figure shredding her shawl. The setting sun caught the glint of moisture in her eyes as she hopelessly extended her arms.

The money meant nothing to her. Slowly she turned around and walked back to the village, crying all the way.

"They have taken my shawl!" she wept and told everyone she

met. "Manjari is cold, Ramprasad is cold," she repeated over and over again.

Someone put another old shawl around her shoulders but she would not accept it saying, "It is not my shawl."

That night she cried and shivered under the tin roof of the tea-stall. She was still there at noon when 11-year-old Bholu returned from school.

He had heard about the incident. He stood and watched Manjari from a distance. She still refused food and drink, just crying and repeating the earlier litany.

Bholu listened to the men and women talking about her.

At 16 years of age, Manjari had lost both parents. From a laughing, playing girl, she suddenly turned into a withdrawn recluse, coming alive only with her pet dog, Ramprasad. Within six months Ramprasad too died. Manjari went into shock and fell seriously ill. The women looked after her but when she recovered, she had become what she was now. The shawl which she always wore had belonged to her mother. Manjari had never parted with it. The shock of losing it had affected her gravely. She was refusing to eat anything.

Upset, Bholu kicked a pebble. He felt angry and ashamed. He was one of those who had teased Manjari the day before.

"O Lord!" he muttered kicking another pebble in his path. It shot out and hit the side of a puppy lying by the roadside. It started yelping.

A puppy's yelp is a very sharp and startling sound. Bholu hurriedly picked up the cringing puppy, trying to quieten it. As the puppy continued to cry, an idea took shape in his mind.

Holding the puppy, he raced to Manjari. "Manjari, Manjari," he gasped, "here is Ramprasad. He is crying. Take him," and he thrust the puppy into her arms. Instinctively, her arms went around it.

For a moment, Manjari looked perplexed, then she said, "You are hurt. My Ramprasad is hurt." She pressed him to her cheek,

stroked and soothed him. In the tender warmth of her arms, the puppy became quiet and started licking her face. "Where have you been all this time?" Manjari continued. "Oh, you are so thin! You have not eaten. Come, I will give you food."

She walked up to the tea-vendor and took the chapatti she had refused earlier. Accepting a cup of tea as well, she dipped pieces of chapatti into it and fed the puppy. In between, she ate some herself. Then she picked up the shawl which she had shrugged off earlier, and wrapped it around herself and the puppy. All activity came to a standstill as everyone watched Manjari. When she returned for another helping, the villagers heaved a sigh of relief.

A smile played on Manjari's face once again.

Bholu, standing some distance away, saw this and felt a lightness in his heart. Surajchand, the grocer, came quietly to his side and tousled his hair. Bholu turned to look up at his face and both smiled.

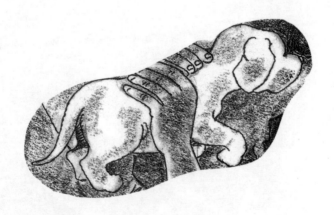

Bholu

Vaneeta Vaid

Lt. Shamsher Pratap Singh's muscles bunched as he sensed the animal creeping through the foliage. His mind raced. He was a soldier trained for combat. But this adversary was different. The worst thing, Shamsher thought, would be to run. No, he had to be on the offensive.

The tiger sneaked into the clearing. Silent and waiting, crouched to pounce.

Never in his wildest imagination had Shamsher foreseen the possibility of this visit by the man-eater which he, with a posse of men, had come to hunt!

Relaxing on a camp chair among the tents, smoking *angeethis* (clay stoves), and surrounding thick jungle, Shamsher had felt good. Days of trekking through the forest to find this spot and setting up camp had been exhausting. Today, in a bid for some peace and quiet, he had sent off his entourage to bathe in the river. Alone, Shamsher had settled down to clean his unloaded rifle, at the same time mentally planning the tiger hunt for the following day. As luck would have it, his uninvited guest decided to call just then.

Shamsher heard the whoosh of air before he actually saw the tiger spring. In one agile movement, Shamsher grasped the rifle and leapt towards the animal. Undeterred, the beast knocked down Shamsher's six foot three inch frame, sending his weapon spiralling away from him.

Pinned, Shamsher kept pushing with all his might at the chest of the tiger. Along with a nameless fear, Shamsher felt a growing quiver of anger, which infused him with strength he never knew he possessed!

Roaring in anticipation of his meal, the tiger lowered his massive head expectantly. Shamsher saw the monster open his jaws, expelling hot, rancid breath, its teeth aiming at his scalp. Shamsher did the only thing he could. He rammed one fist deep down the tiger's throat. Then getting a hand on its spiky tongue, Shamsher pulled. Before the gagging tiger could chomp at his hand, Shamsher managed to extricate it. With superhuman power, he gripped the brute's front paws, at the same time curling his jodhpured and high boots-encased legs around its belly. They both rolled.

For Shamsher it was a losing battle. He was weakening, his hold slackening.

Just then, there was a flurry of movement and a blur. The tiger was slapped off him.

Dizzy and battered, still sprawled on the ground, Shamsher vaguely sensed another presence. Groggily he tried to sit up. Was that a bear grappling with the tiger? Not possible, was Shamsher 's last thought as he sank into a haze of blackness.

*　　　　　*　　　　　*

Mool Singh, Shamsher's valet, grunted as he bent to lift the oil lamp he had been lighting and hang it on a nail on the tent pole inside.

"Why did I go off for a bath? I should not have listened to Saab..." he muttered to himself.

116

"I would have whipped your hide for disobeying orders."

Mool Singh whirled around and rushed to the single cot in the tent. "The Lord be praised! Saabji, you are finally awake. We gave you up as dead!" Mool Singh looked away to hide the glisten of tears.

'I would have been but...' Shamsher thought. No, it could not have been a bear which rescued him. He could have been dreaming! It must have been Mool Singh.

"Thanks for saving my life, old chap. How did you manage to slap the tiger aside?"

"Yes, the tiger is dead," answered Mool Singh not quite following Shamsher's question "Now no more talking, Saabji. Let me apply this poultice on you, then I shall get you milk with turmeric in it!"

Shamsher's mind was screaming for answers, yet Mool Singh's ministrations were too comforting to ignore. He shut his mind and settled back.

The next evening, Shamsher managed to hobble out of the tent to sit near the fire stoked by Mool Singh for him. Mool Singh issued a series of instructions to the scurrying helpers, then finally squatted on the ground to massage his beloved Saabji's feet.

Coming home after his army commission for the first time, Shamsher was greeted by a *haveli* rife with wild stories about a man-eater which was terrorizing the woodcutters in the jungle. Since *Bade Sarkar* (the senior master), Shamsher's father, was out on an extended hunting trip elsewhere, everyone looked towards *Chote Sarkar* (the junior master) to do something!

Like his father, the famous hunter and *Jagirdar* (landlord) of hereabouts, Shamsher felt the pull of the jungle, on the periphery of which he had grown up. This trip was meant to fulfil the desire which had plagued him ever since his father promised him permission to hunt only after the completion of his education and commission.

So here he was with a team of men from his father's grounds, plus tribals as guides.

Glancing down at his faithful valet's bent head, Shamsher once again repeated his inquiry, "How did you manage to slap and kill that beast of a tiger aside, Mool Singhji?"

"Kill what tiger, Saabji? The dead one? Me, kill it? No, Saabji. We wondered about that when we found you all mauled and crumpled on a bed of dry leaves. You had passed out. What surprised us was that your wounds were clean, as if someone had licked them! We assumed it was a bear attack judging by the fresh bear pug marks all over!" His voice trailed off at Shamsher's sudden straightening.

"What? A bear? Did you say a bear?" Shamsher asked. He crushed Mool Singh's shoulders and whispered, "Bholu! He saved me! Bholu came to me!"

The name pierced through Shamsher's head, exposing thoughts buried under layers of guilt, pain and torment, best forgotten. It all came back to him. Oh, no! Shamsher clutched his head.

"What happened, Saabji? Who is Bholu?" asked Mool Singh.

Dry mouthed, yet with memories bursting to be shared, Shamsher stared unseeingly ahead and began to speak. Years fell away. Shamsher was once again a child.

*   *   *

Suppressed excitement rolled through the corridors of the *haveli*. *Bade Sarkar* was back! After months in the jungle on a hunting trip, he had returned.

Twelve-year-old Shamsher could hardly contain himself when he received summons for an audience with his father. He was even more excited when his nurse guided him towards the backyard and not the usual *baithak* (parlour).

"Aaah, Shamsher Pratapji," his father greeted him. "Come, come, see what we have for you here!"

In the centre of the ring of people milling the courtyard, Shamsher saw a frightened, cowering bear cub. He waited for his father to speak.

"This is for you. We found it beside its dead mother. He is your responsibility now. Groom and nurture him as you would a younger brother!"

Signalling to someone in the small crowd of servants, he barked, "Jai Singhji, you will assist *Chote Sarkar* in bringing up this cub."

Here began a friendship. Shamsher spent most of his free time with Bholu, a name coined by Jai Singh on seeing the cub's pathetic expression.

Within no time, Bholu grew to a monstrous size with an equally monstrous appetite! Their best times were spent at the half dried river bed. Jai Singh was a merry companion.

As time flew, Bholu became restless. Never chained, he was given a free run of a fenced compound. However, like an adolescent, his instincts drove him to want to abandon discipline and taste life as it had meant to have been for him. He would gaze for hours over the fence at the dark forest encircling the *haveli*.

Soon Bholu was breaking the fencing and escaping to the cluster of tenancies outside. First his raids on food were laughed off. He was always caught and brought back. Then he began swiping his claws at everyone but Shamsher. Even Jai Singh was not spared.

Somehow Shamsher managed to dilute the incident and Bholu was not punished. Complaints flowed in to *Chote Sarkar*.

Still Shamsher was totally unprepared when Jai Singh interrupted his studies one day and announced, "*Bade Sarkar* has remembered *Chote Sarkar*."

The teacher nodded permission.

With a feeling of dread at Jai Singh's closed features, Shamsher nervously followed him to his father's presence.

His stomach dipped in fear at the sight of a grim-faced Mr. Heath, the representative of the British Resident, seated opposite his father.

"Mr. Heath Saab has come with a grievous charge against your bear," began his father. "Apparently your bear has been terrorizing one and all for sometime?"

The emphasis on "your" was not lost on Shamsher. He lowered his eyes guiltily.

His father continued, "This morning he broke through their fencing and hugged their pet dog to its death."

Shamsher's gasp was lost in the subsequent words, "No, this won't do. I have two options. One, to shoot it. Two, to banish it into the jungles across the river towards the mountains. What do you suggest?"

Shamsher was tongue-tied. From the corner of his eye he saw Mr. Heath leaning forward.

"Yes?" his father prompted.

Squashing the impulse to scream, reason or protest, since it went against the rules of his royal upbringing, Shamsher just managed to mumble, "Banish him, Sir!"

Once out of the room Shamsher ran all the way to Bholu. Flinging himself at the delighted bear, Shamsher wept into Bholu's rough fur. Bholu was dismayed at his friend's sorrow. Whimpering, he began to perform all the tricks taught to him in an attempt to make Shamsher giggle.

Shamsher smiled weakly, knowing that the grief in his heart could never go away.

At four in the morning they came to take away Bholu. But all attempts to harness him failed. Finally Jai Singh roused Shamsher who, after an exhausting bout of tears, had fallen into a dreamless slumber.

Seeing his friend, Bholu emitted a welcoming and relieved grunt. He complained to Shamsher about the treatment he was getting.

Holding his huge pal close, Shamsher lost control. "No, no, go away, no one shall take Bholu away!"

He ranted and raved but when Jai Singh hissed, "You can't go against *Bade Sarkar's* orders, *Chote Sarkar*," his protests died. Tears flowing freely, Shamsher buried his face into Bholu's chest. Then, without turning, he extended his hand for the collar and the harness.

Bholu shocked scream tore into Shamsher. Shaking and twisting yet unable to shake off the choking collar, Bholu stretched towards Shamsher.

Shamsher turned and took a step backwards.

Then all the fight seemed to leave Bholu. He just stood there awhile staring shortsightedly at Shamsher. With one last look at his friend, Bholu allowed himself to be led away.

*   *   *

"We never saw him again and all I remember is wailing and calling his name for a long, long time..." sighed Lt. Shamsher Pratap Singh.

"It was the expression on Bholu's face..." Shamsher said more to himself than to Mool Singh. "With a child's instinct I could feel his body language telling me that he would have never let anyone take me away!

"Day in and day out I kept thinking how lame a friend I had been. It went against all the values and grooming imparted to me. Why hadn't I had the guts to stand up to my father in protest? Why so many tears for a beast, I would been asked. No, Bholu was not a beast. He had been my friend who had trusted me, and I had let him down."

Mool Singh watched his young master with a stab of anxiety and despair. He was full of idealism, he had so much more life to taste. But the lessons of life were not always kind.

The fire had died and moon fully risen. There was nothing left to be said. Shamsher limped stiffly back into the tent.

An undercurrent of sadness seemed to sweep the camp the following day. The man-eater had been identified and was dead. Their mission was over. Eventually orders were given to pack.

"Coming in a moment," acknowledged Shamsher when Mool Singh announced that they were ready to move.

Shamsher took one last look around, then wandered to where the thick jungle began, a little beyond the camp. Staring into its green fingers of foliage, Shamsher whispered, "Bholu, forgive me..." Feeling foolish and self-conscious, Shamsher made a move to leave.

A rustle arrested his attention. Shamsher's heart beat faster.

Almost as if in slow motion, a bear revealed itself from behind the screen of plants.

Shamsher and the bear stood staring at each other, frozen in the enormity of the moment, none making an attempt to get closer to the other.

"Saabji, Saabji!" Mool Singh's worried call broke the spell.

The bear shook itself, moved backwards and melted into the jungle.

"Bholu has forgiven me," ran a jubilant cry in Shamsher's mind. He felt it! Along with that thought came another one. Bholu's shortsighted gaze conveyed something else—he was happy where he was. This was where he belonged, in this wilderness, where his spirit ran wild and independent.

"Goodbye, dear friend, it is time to move on!" Shamsher remembered the lines softly.

With that he turned around and walked towards the waiting men. A weight had lifted off him—his guilt and pain had vanished.

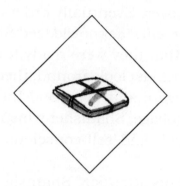

A Soldier's Son
Shobha Ghose

The plane was veering and shuddering in the sky. It was like a winged bird fluttering and fighting to keep its balance in a last, desperate attempt to continue flying. It was losing height rapidly and hurtling towards earth. It would be a matter of minutes before it crashed. A figure fell out of the fiery object that was plummetting down to earth. A white structure mushroomed and opened like a flower in the sky and a figure floated gently down with the wind to the ground.

A small boy emerged from the clump of trees a short distance away. He had been watching the plane for some time. He had seen it being shot down by enemy fire and the pilot parachute down from the flaming plane. He came out from the darkness of the trees. The next moment something flashed across the intervening space and the little boy, ten or twelve years old, had reached the wounded pilot.

"Come with me, Sir. The enemy will be here any minute. There is no time to lose. There is an army camp near by. You will be safe there."

The pilot staggered to his feet, took two or three faltering

124

steps and collapsed to the ground. "I can't walk. My legs are probably fractured. Can you do something for me?"

The child could see it was with great effort that the man could talk. "Yes, Sir, I will do anything you want."

"You are small. Better take a chance," he muttered under his breath.

"Not a chance, Sir, a certainty. What do you want me to do?"

The man's hands were bleeding. He fumbled clumsily inside his pocket and took out a packet of papers. "Take this to the Commanding Officer of the army unit," he said. "Tell him this must reach the Air Force Station, Ambala, by night. Tell him to take care of it and make sure it reaches Ambala on time. Now run for your life and your country. You must avoid the enemy. WIll you able be to do it?"

"Yes, Sir, I will do it. But you? The enemy will catch you."

"Don't worry about me. I can't escape. I will try and distract them. You run and hand over the packet."

"Yes, Sir," said the boy with a smart salute.

The man could not help smiling although he was grimacing with the pain of his injuries. He began to crawl away from the boy in the opposite direction.

The small figure streaked across the open space, back to the trees from which it had emerged. The enemy, however, had seen him. A few of them gave chase and shot at him. The cartridges fell everywhere around him. The child ran fast and was lost to sight. The enemy gave up and turned their attention to the crawling figure of the pilot.

A few minutes later, the little boy stood at the sentry post of the army unit. "Take me to the Commander Saheb. There is something I have to deliver to him."

"Little boy, you cannot go to the Commander Saheb. No one is allowed to go to his room unless it is very important."

"What I have is very important. It is from the pilot whose plane was shot down."

"You mean the plane that just crashed? A rescue party has gone to look for him."

"Yes, I had gone there to bring him back to safety. The enemy was after him. He was injured and couldn't walk. He gave me a packet to be delivered to the Commander Saheb immediately."

The sentry searched the boy. He allowed him the search but held on to the bloodstained packet.

"It is urgent, I tell you. The pilot is badly injured and can't walk at all. The enemy will take him away and torture him. I must see the Commander Saheb. I must give him this packet. I must guide him to the officer and show him where the enemy lines are."

"All right."

The sentry picked up the field telephone and spoke into it. A sepoy came to the sentry post and with a curt, "Follow me," moved ahead to a Nissen hut.

He entered, followed by the boy and, standing to attention, saluted. The little boy did the same. Everyone stared at him.

"Come here. Why did you want to see me?" the Commanding Officer asked.

"The pilot from the plane which was shot down gave me this packet to be delivered to you, Sir. He told me to tell you that it must reach the Air Force Station, Ambala, by night."

"I see. And who are you?"

My name is Maqbool Butt. My father was awarded a medal for bravery. He died fighting for the nation. My mother and I live here now. I was watching the plane when I heard an anti-aircraft gun fire and saw the plane become unsteady. I saw him fall to the ground. I knew I must save him. The enemy was just a little distance away. I ran to bring him back by a short cut. When I reached him, I found that he could not walk. He was bleeding profusely. He told me not to worry about him, but to try and get this packet to you and tell you that it must reach Ambala tonight. It is very important."

127

"Son, you are very brave. Weren't you afraid of the enemy?"

"My father told me never to be afraid of any enemy. They can't do a thing if your number is not written on the bullet."

The Commanding Officer smiled. "Has the enemy been able to catch the pilot?"

"I don't know, Sir. I couldn't wait to see. I had to carry out my orders first. I know where he fell. I also know where the enemy lines are. I can guide you to it by a short cut so that you can intercept them and cut off their retreat."

"Good! You are indeed the brave son of a brave soldier."

"We must go at once, Sir. The enemy came on foot. If you take jeeps you will be able to surround them and catch them."

"Instructions noted, Sir, action will be taken," smiled the Commanding Officer.

Five minutes later the group of enemy soldiers found themselves surrounded by jeeps. There was no escape. One of them started to run but realized that it was of no use. Throwing down his gun he raised his hands above his head.

The enemy was rounded up and the pilot rescued. He was bleeding for he had been dragged along when he failed to rise and walk even when prodded with bayonets. He was muttering something incoherently, "Boy...packet..." He could say no more.

"Take him to the Military Hospital at once. Easy does it. Don't jerk him. Ask Major Dogra to accompany him. He needs a doctor. Maqbool, thank you, my brave son. Now you must be taken home. Your mother will be worried about you."

"I am Maqbool Butt, son of India. These are my brothers and this is my land. It is here that I was born and nurtured. My father's blood is mixed with the soil of this land and my mother's tears water the earth on which our crops grow. My loyalty rests here with my brothers, blood relations of the soil, for we have broken bread on the same land."

The boy who had been standing, crumpled up all of a sudden and fell down.

"Maqbool, what is it? Are you hurt, my son?"

"Only a scratch, Sir. The enemy fire hit my leg." The blood from the wound fell on the ground, reddening the earth on which it fell. The child looked with wonder at the blood dripping from the wound.

"My father's blood has fallen and mingled with this soil and now my blood also has fallen on the same soil. My parents will have reason to be proud of me."

The Commanding Officer gathered the fallen figure in his arms and carried the child to the ambulance. He laid him gently down on the stretcher.

The boy stirred and grimaced with pain. Major Dogra moved swiftly to him and gently eased his leg into a more comfortable position.

"Is the child hurt badly?" The Commanding Officer frowned in worry. His eyes brimmed with tears.

Maqbool smiled through his dirt-streaked face. "A soldier never weeps, Sir."

Another voice, from somewhere far away, lost in the distant years, seemed to say, "A soldier never runs from the enemy, father, you told me so. He must face the bullets even when they tear his chest to shreds."

"Yes, my son, a soldier must not weep, but a father's heart weeps and bleeds with the blood of his son. I received the P.V.C. for my son in the 1971 war."

"He must have been very brave. You too are very brave. Sir. Don't worry, I will be all right. I am a soldier's son and I too will become a soldier when I grow up."

"You, my child, are a soldier already. We are proud of you and hope that some day you will lead our army with the same daring and courage that you have shown today."

A Different Diwali
Tithi Tavora

Alok watched Chinamma scrape the coconuts. After Chinamma finished, she always gave him a little coconut to eat. But, today, Chinamma was crying. Every once in a while she dabbed at her eyes with the end of her faded sari.

"Why are you crying, Chinamma?" Alok asked.

"Nothing, *Baba* (child), nothing," said Chinamma, getting up to put away the plate of grated coconut.

"Aren't you going to give me some coconut to eat?" asked Alok anxiously.

"Oh! yes! I forgot," said Chinamma, popping some into his waiting mouth. She smiled faintly.

It was only when Mummy came that Chinamma told them the cause of her grief.

"There has been an explosion at the cracker factory where my children work, *Amma*. Seven children died..." She was sobbing openly now. "My son, he managed to run out, but my little girl..."

Alok did not want to hear more. He could not bear it! His hands flew to cover his ears. Through them he heard her muffled voice continue, "...she was saved...her hands are badly burnt. The cracker she was packing exploded in her hands."

Alok lowered his hands from his ears in relief. At least it was not what he had feared! She was not dead!

He knew Chinamma's daughter. Until last year, she used to come with her mother on Sundays. Then, when Chinamma went to her village in summer, she came back without the girl. He remembered Mummy scolding her, "Why did you stop her studies and leave her there?"

Chinamma had replied, "*Amma*, we have to repay the loan we took to repair our house. They pay well at the factory. Many children from the village work there. Besides, her brother is also working there. He will keep an eye on her."

Mummy had been quite annoyed with Chinamma. Now the little girl was hurt.

"Where is she now?" asked Mummy.

"In hospital. The doctors say she needs very expensive medicines. How much more money can I borrow from people?"

Chinamma sounded so helpless, Alok felt he had to do something to help her. He saw Mummy press some money into Chinamma's hands and suddenly he had an idea! He ran up to his room and felt inside the old wallet that Papa had let him have. His fingers pulled out a hundred-rupee note. Papa had given it to him to buy crackers for Diwali. He held it for a minute, then ran down and handed the note to Chinamma. "Take this," he said. "For your daughter's medicines."

Chinamma was moved. She would not accept the money till Alok's mother persuaded her to do so. When she left, his mother hugged Alok and said, "That was very sweet of you, darling."

"It is only one hundred rupees, Mummy. It will not be enough. I wish I could give her more," said Alok sadly.

"Yes," nodded his mother with a sigh. "So do I, but it is Diwali and we have many expenses. It is difficult to spare more. Anyway, we did the best we could."

Alok was not satisfied. The image of poor Chinamma crying kept troubling him.

In the park that evening, all the children were discussing Chinamma's daughter's accident. They felt sorry for Chinamma. They were all fond of her. She had been working in their colony for many years, and most of the children knew her since they were toddlers. Seeing everyone's concern, Alok suddenly knew what they could do.

"Listen," he said, "what if we all pool in the money our parents give us to buy crackers, and give it all to Chinamma for her daughter's treatment? I already gave her my cracker money, but it is not enough."

His idea was greeted by silence.

"You mean, instead of buying crackers, we should give her the money?" asked Deepa doubtfully.

"Exactly," said Alok.

"What fun is Diwali without crackers?" objected Deepak.

"How can we have fun when that poor girl is lying in hospital? Besides, there is more to Diwali than crackers," replied Alok.

"Three cheers for the martyr!" mocked Deepak.

"Don't be nasty, Deepak," rebuked Roshan. "I think Alok's idea is a brilliant one."

Everybody fell silent. Roshan was the eldest amongst them. They usually went along with whatever he said.

"After all," continued Roshan, "we are partly responsible for what happened to Chinamma's daughter."

"How is that?" asked Jyoti, puzzled.

"Look at it this way," explained Roshan. "If no one bought crackers, there wouldn't be any need for cracker factories. The question of anyone getting injured would not arise."

"I love crackers!" wailed Chirag.

"Besides," persisted Roshan, "think of how often Chinamma has helped us in the past."

"Yes," admitted Chirag. "Last year, during Mummy's

operation, she came and stayed with me."

"And the time the mad dog chased me on the way to school, she didn't even bother about herself. She came running to save mefrom the beast," reminisced Deepa.

"Can't we do at least this much for her? Sacrifice a few crackers?" pressed Alok seeing that everyone was beginning to have a change of heart.

"Yes, and what are crackers anyway, just causing air and noise pollution, leaving the streets dirty," opined Jyoti. She secretly liked the plan for quite another reason—she was terrified of crackers!

"Not to mention the injuries they cause," added Roshan.

"That is final then," declared Alok, "we all bring in our money tomorrow and give it to Chinamma."

Everybody agreed except Deepak who stubbornly refused to understand how anyone could celebrate Diwali without crackers. The rest decided to ignore him and went home feeling strangely happy.

The next evening, when Chinamma walked past the park on her way home, the children called out to her. Roshan went up to her and handed her the bundle of money they had collected. It was almost two thousand rupees. "Chinamma, take this for your daughter's treatment. All of us have collected it for you," he said.

At first, Chinamma refused to take the money. "No, *Baba*, no! How can I take money from you children?" she exclaimed in horror. Nothing the children said would convince her.

Finally, it was left to Alok's mother to convince Chinamma to accept the money.

She looked at all of them with eyes full of tears as she took the money. "God bless all of you!" she said in a choked voice before hurrying on her way home.

The next few days passed quickly in a flurry of activity. Everybody was busy getting ready for Diwali—cleaning the

house, preparing sweets, making *rangolis* (traditional floor decorations with rice flour)... And then it was Diwali! All the families gathered in the park to celebrate it together. In appreciation of what the children had done for Chinamma, their fathers had organized a gala evening. There was to be a magic show which the children were particularly looking forward to.

As they waited for the show to begin, Jyoti suddenly said, "Look! Chinamma has brought her daughter!"

Indeed, there, hiding behind Chinamma's sari, stood a little girl. Her hands were swathed in bandages but she was smiling brightly.

The children crowded around her. "How is she now?"

"She is much better," replied Chinamma. "She has been discharged from the hospital. Thanks to you children!"

Suddenly, to everybody's surprise, Deepak came up to the girl and handed her a lovely new doll.

"What is this, Deepak?" asked Roshan. "We thought you would be busy lighting your crackers."

"I changed my mind," said Deepak sheepishly. "It is not much fun playing with them alone anyway."

Chinamma's daughter admired her new doll. It was difficult to decide what shone brightest that evening, the joy on Chinamma's face, the beaming faces of the children or the pride in their parents' eyes. One thing was certain, though, as the magician later said, "In the whole of Delhi there isn't a colony that glows brighter this Diwali than this one."

Upside Down Magic
Sonali Bhatia

It was the first day of the Diwali holidays. Malvika was playing in the garden with her kitten, Billi. They were playing hide-and-seek. Malvika was always the 'seeker', since Billi knew how to hide quite well, but could not search for Malvika if she hid. Malvika did not mind not getting a chance to hide throughout the game. It was fun to explore the garden thinking, 'If I were a little kitten, where would I hide myself?'

She found herself crawling beneath the hibiscus bush, searching for a sign of Billi. Suddenly, she thought she saw Billi's tail peeping out from under a small pile of leaves. She reached out and grabbed it, exclaiming triumphantly, "Got you!"

To Malvika's astonishment, she heard a small, squeaky voice plead, "Please, little girl, let me go!"

When she drew her hand out, still clutching what she had thought was a tail, she found it was, in fact, the tiny leg of a little fairy!

Malvika was amazed. So amazed that she did not even turn the poor fairy the right way round. She just held her by the leg, upside down, and stared and stared.

136

She saw a tiny, brown-haired girl, the size of her smallest doll. The girl had black eyes, a cute snub nose and ears that stuck out a bit. The most fascinating thing about her was a pair of silvery-pink wings, like the wings of a dragonfly. In her right hand, she clutched a magic wand—a stick that gleamed in all the colours of the rainbow.

Malvika found her voice at last. "Are you...are you really a fairy?" she whispered.

"Yes. And now that you have found me, I must grant you three wishes, since that is the rule," replied the fairy.

"Three wishes! You mean I can ask for anything I want?" gasped Malvika.

"That is right, Malvika. But you are holding me upside down, so the magic will work upside down," the fairy answered.

"Upside down?" Malvika was really puzzled. "What is upside down magic, fairy?"

The fairy explained. "Remember, Malvika, when you want something to happen, you must wish for the opposite. Then you will get what you really want! If you wish for what you actually want, the opposite will happen. That is upside down magic. It gives you the opposite of anything after you say, 'I wish...' Understand?"

With that, the fairy disappeared.

Malvika stayed under the hibiscus bush for a minute, too surprised to move. A plaintive "Meow" brought her out of her daze. Billi was rubbing against her, mewing for her to continue the game.

Malvika picked up the kitten in excitement. "Oh, Billi, the most wonderful thing just happened! I met a fairy! You know, she has granted me three upside down wishes. I must remember to wish for exactly the opposite of what I want. I really must tell Avani about this." Still clutching Billi, the excited little girl ran to the other end of the garden, where the wall joined her neighbour, Avani's garden.

138

"Avani, Avani," called Malvika loudly, "come here. I have some great news!"

Avani came running up and, before Malvika could continue, she exclaimed, "Hey, Malvika, guess what! My granny is coming to visit us tomorrow, and Mummy is letting me make the *idlis* (a preparation made of rice) for her breakfast. Granny loves *idlis*, and I have been learning how to make them so that they come out nice and soft and fluffy. Now I'm going to make them for granny. Isn't that great?"

"That is fabulous, Avani. I wish that your *idlis*..."

Here Malvika stopped speaking. She had said the words, "I wish..." The upside down magic was at work. She had to say the opposite of what she wanted Avani's *idlis* to turn out to be. Oh, dear! She had not even told Avani about the upside down magic yet. She sighed, and, in a low voice, continued, "I wish that your *idlis* turn out to be tasteless and as hard as rocks!"

Avani was shocked. Malvika was her best friend, and here she was wishing that Avani's *idlis* turned out badly! Avani burst into tears and ran back home, before Malvika could explain.

Malvika groaned, and cuddled Billi sadly. "Oh, Billi! Now Avani is upset with me. She will not even let me explain! I have quarrelled with my best friend all because I met a fairy."

Then she cheered up a little, "Anyway, at least Avani's granny will have delicious, soft *idlis* to eat because of the magic. That will make Avani very glad."

Feeling a little comforted by this thought, Malvika walked back to her house to tell her mother and her little brother, Kunal, of her morning's adventure, and explain all about the upside down magic.

Kunal was playing in the garden with a lovely, big red-and-green balloon shaped like a butterfly. He had won it as a prize in a fancy dress contest, and was very proud of it.

Kunal was so intent on looking up at the balloon that he did not notice where he was going. He tripped over one of the flowerpots, and, as he fell, the string of the balloon slipped out of his grasp. A little gust of wind grabbed the balloon and took it away merrily. Poor little Kunal burst into tears, and their mother came running out of the house to comfort him.

Malvika, watching all this, knew what she had to do. Use up one more of her three precious wishes, of course. Only, it was an upside down wish, and she had not even told her mother about it yet. She had already used up one of her wishes, and now she was about to use another, before she had even mentioned her great adventure to anyone. Anyway, it could not be helped. Kunal's balloon was still in sight. There was no time to waste. If she had to use magic to get it back for him, she had to do so immediately, before the balloon disappeared.

She wished, "I wish that Kunal's beautiful balloon never comes back!"

The direction of the wind changed suddenly. The balloon, which had been just a little dot in the sky, started looking larger. Soon, Malvika, Kunal and their mother could clearly see the butterfly shape and the red and green colours of the balloon. Two minutes after Malvika had wished, the balloon had landed safely in Kunal's lap, and he was hugging it in joy. The upside down magic had worked wonderfully well!

But Malvika's mother was very, very angry with her. "Shame on you, Malvika!" she shouted. "I know you did not win a prize in the fancy dress contest yourself, but you can't be jealous of Kunal in this way! Imagine wishing that he loses his lovely prize! Just for that, I will not give you any of the *payasam* (a sweet dish) I made this morning."

Malvika's mother picked Kunal up and marched into the house, not heeding poor Malvika's shouts and pleas.

Malvika felt sad. Two precious wishes gone, Avani upset, her mother furious. She sat in the shade of the gulmohar tree, buried her face in Billi's soft fur, and wept for a long time. "Oh, Billi! What am I do to?" she wailed.

Billi mewed and tried to lick her with her tiny pink tongue.

Suddenly, Malvika had an idea. The only way out of the situation seemed to be to use up her third, cherished wish. She could wish that her mother and Avani would let her explain. It would have to be an upside down wish, too. What a waste! It would be her last, and she had not even wished for that lovely doll she had seen at the toy shop, or the paint set she wanted, like the one Avani had. There was no other answer.

Malvika wished, "I wish Mummy and Avani will continue to be angry with me, and will never let me explain what happened."

Just then, she heard a shout. It was her mother calling her into the house. She ran in eagerly.

Her mother was holding out the telephone receiver to her. "Avani's mother on the phone for you, dear."

"Malvika," she heard Hina Aunty say on the telephone, "Avani told me what happened. I am sure you didn't mean what you said. Would you like to come over rightaway and help make the *idli* batter?"

"Of course, I would, Hina Aunty," responded Malvika, delighted. "I will tell you the whole story then."

She replaced the receiver and turned to her mother, who was smiling at her. The magic had worked again—Mummy was no longer angry.

"Are you going to Avani's house, dear?" Mummy asked.

"Yes, Mummy, but before that I have something to tell you." Malvika related the happenings of the morning to her mother and Kunal. "...you see, Mummy, I was not being jealous of Kunal. I was actually using a wish for him," she finished.

"Well, I am sorry I was angry, dear, but you must understand what it sounded like to me, at that time," said Mummy, hugging her. "Now run along to Avani's and explain things to her, too."

Explain she did, and Avani was thrilled that her *idlis* would be magic ones! "Thank you for using your wish on me, Malvika," Avani exclaimed. "Sorry I got upset with you!"

Avani was so elated about being able to serve perfect, magic *idlis*, that she gifted her paint set to Malvika, and Mummy was so proud of her for using a wish for her little brother that she bought the lovely doll for her.

All that Malvika has to say now is, "If you meet a fairy, you must not hold her upside down."

Of Flowers and Flying Through the Year
Brinda Gill

Below a cold, grey sky of early January, my black and yellow autorickshaw, akin to a jumbo bumble-bee, droned madly around the Shantipath roundabout.

"Circle it once more," I urged the bewildered driver, "for the fragrance of the devil tree is irresistible."

"What do you mean?" he demanded.

As if answering his query, the autorickshaw floated weightlessly off the road, slowly shaped into a bumble-bee heading directly and uncontrollably towards the tree's sweet cinnamon-scented flowers. The flying start nudged the shocked driver off the vehicle, but I held on tightly and was immediately indulged to a bee's-eye view of the capital city.

Bumble-Bee drank deftly from the tiny flowers within a dark, private world meshed by foliage. "That was very nice," he said wandering into the nearby Mahavir Park. "To me some segments of the ridge are reminiscent of the spontaneous forests and natural clearings eulogized in our mythology, an ideal tryst for separated lovers, where a fragile maiden hastens to meet her beloved some stormy night or where Sri Krishna played his flute...the fragrance of the coral jasmine or devil tree suffusing the senses. I love the solitude of these untamed areas, the beauty of the trees as they stand silent for months and suddenly burst into bloom."

After a refreshing rest, Bumble-Bee took off. "Each month brings a discrete flush of flowers with it. In February, the Mughal Gardens are at their best," he buzzed joyously, landing on a flamboyant double dahlia beside the stone pergola there. Then he flew straight to the Round Garden Pool, circled by tiers of brilliant flowers, ascending the circular slopes around the Pool where many of his brethren were amicably and noisily drinking from the bountiful flowers.

"There is always plenty for all, so why waste time arguing?" he said dreamily. "These gardens complete the splendour of the President's residence. I have heard the gardeners here reminiscing of the old British days. So many distinct moods and time frames co-exist in our green spaces...giving us much to choose from."

Then flying past the bustling crossroads of Dhaula Kuan to the sleepy, green roads of the Cantonment, Bumble-Bee settled down on a large silk cotton tree full of flowers, crows, mynas, flower-peckers, bulbuls and sunbirds. "*Semuls* are hard to come by in the newer areas of Delhi as the city continually adds concentric dimensions," he said disappearing into a sumptuous crimson flower. "Next month the cotton buds will burst. In the old days the silky, soft cotton was stuffed into pillow cases."

After a leisurely stay at the *semul* he buzzed through bauhinia trees, speckled with purple, deep pink or white flowers as their camel hoof-shaped leaves tossed in the cool March breeze.

A few sips later Bumble-Bee abruptly flew through a clump of trees, as if he was being led by his nose, to a tree smothered with mango blossoms. "If these blooming flowers are any indication of the fruit to follow, we should have a merry feast this summer," he sang tottering through the trees.

144

By then the air was warm and dry. "T.S. Eliot may have had his reasons for remarking that April is a cruel month, but I, for one, am sure he never saw an April in Delhi. Just look..." he gestured towards the bougainvillea cascading down garden walls, their colourful bracts adding life to dry apartment blocks, and a jacaranda tree full of fragile, blue-violet flowers standing serenely by the road.

"Before you can have your fill of it, blooms the gulmohar," he buzzed darting between its large, scarlet clusters.

"Then it is time for the laburnum to show off, splashing itself with golden-yellow drooping flower bunches. I always put on weight this month," he confessed between gulps.

The June heat was relentless and exhausting. Bumble-Bee said the best place to rest was in the shade of the short jarul trees, their crowns studded with large, mauve panicles. We flew through the cool avenues of central Delhi where, even before the roads were readied, Sir Lutyens had large, slow-growing trees planted to hem in the sides, Bumble-Bee had been told by his grandfather.

We descended at Nehru Park. The varied flora of the park offered much respite from the heat while in the cool of the evenings, Bumble-Bee buzzed off to mango trees to drink in the sweet juice dribbling from the fruit. This is life, he would say, thanking the Creator manifold for 'the delights of life', as he called them.

A few pre-monsoon clouds darkened the sky one afternoon. They were enough to make Bumble-Bee fly off to Humayun's Tomb. "The Mughal Gardens provide a completely different charm with their formal, geometrical patterns taking on the lines of the monuments they ensconse. Away from the bustle of the city, I love to spend a rainy afternoon here in the *neems,* tamarinds, *maulsaris.*"

He rambled on about how, occasionally, on a Sunday, he would fly off to the green university area, sometimes keep

company with the lonely marble men standing amidst *keekars* at the northern-most tip of Delhi. He meant the British public commemorative statues at Coronation Ground. The fragrance of the small, yellow, globular *keekar* clusters as rain dampened the dry earth was a heady mix, he said.

During the monsoons that followed, Bumble-Bee stayed warm and snug in yellow oleanders and yellow elder trees whose blooms stood out beautifully against a darkened sky. These were abundantly flowering, plentiful in Delhi Development Authority-built residential areas, as the cassias and gulmohars nearby stood silent; the flowering *chandini, madhumati, champa* and *mogra* added by the residents livened the uniform, low skyline.

Bumble-Bee was quite happy. "The city has consciously brought in smaller flowering trees with apartment blocks. Obviously you cannot grow a banyan tree here even if you wished to. I don't mind these smaller trees, but my sting has gone rusty for hardly any children disturb me while I am drinking at the flowers. These are not trees they can climb. What greater joy for a child than to select, test and swing from the aerial root of a banyan. Now when I was really young...

"Let us go to the rusty shield-bearer, though it blooms mainly in March. I normally visit it during its second blush in October."

It was a handsome tree with pyramid-shaped flowers, reddish-brown pods sprinkled around its feathery crown. The days passed leisurely amongst its foliage.

The heady fragrance of the coral jasmine blooming through the cool, early winter nights caused Bumble-Bee to be a little intoxicated on rising, but by mid-morning he would be back on wing.

"We must hasten," he announced one morning for he had heard that the corisia were in bloom.

We passed a siris tree, its thousand golden-yellow bean pods lit by slanting sunrays, a light breeze causing them to whisper some primeval secret amongst themselves', according to Bumble-Bee.

He buzzed straight towards the corisia dotting the roundabout near Kamraj Marg. The leafless trees studded with pink and white flowers were a feast for the eyes. After a quick gaze at them he plunged into the flowers, pausing only to move between the blooms. He was definitely overdoing it, despite my discreet pleas. He drank till he dropped, but was giddily lifted into a thermal, spiralling madly towards the sky when it was suddenly lost and we came reeling down...right at the Shanti Path roundabout.

Bumble-Bee had a soft landing—not as a bee, but as an autorickshaw. And who should be there but its stunned driver.

"Where have you been?" he cried.

"A journey through time and space," I smiled dreamily.

He peered into the petrol tank. It was tanked up with a fragrant fuel! He looked at the meter—it showed an astronomical figure. I was aghast. It was his turn to smile as he blissfully sang, "...flights of fancy do not come at down to earth prices..."

He patted his vehicle saying, "You seem to have been busy as a bee."

The autorickshaw hiccuped noisily. The driver yanked the starter and, dodging vehicles, we careened crazily into clogged city streets as I wondered if this wonderful flight had been a dream. As I held on to my belongings I saw a corisia flower lying next to me on the seat.

CBT's Other Short Story Collections

Short Stories for Children

More Short Stories for Children

Some More Short Stories for Children

Read-aloud Stories

24 Short Stories

Kidnapped and Other Stories

Kaleidoscope
34 Short Stories

CBT's Golden Set

Stories from Panchatantra

Tales from Indian Classics

Treasury of Indian Tales

Folk Tales Retold

Marar Mouse and Other Stories

Stories of India
Mrinalini Sarabhai

Adventure Stories
Arup Kumar Dutta

The Story of Writing
Nita Berry

Animal World
*A. David
Shivakumar*

CBT's Select Fiction

Adventures Two
Cheryl Rao

The Biratpur Adventure
Mitra Phukan

The Twins' Holiday Adventure
Priti Banerjee

The Virus Trap
Ira Saxena

Kusum
Dipavali Debroy

The Fiery Cross
A.K. Srikumar

Life with Grandfather
Shankar